MW01393335

OTHER PEOPLE

GEORGE FITHEN

WestBow
PRESS
A DIVISION OF THOMAS NELSON

Copyright © 2013 George Fithen.

All rights reserved. No part of this book may be used or reproduced by any means, graphic, electronic, or mechanical, including photocopying, recording, taping or by any information storage retrieval system without the written permission of the publisher except in the case of brief quotations embodied in critical articles and reviews.

WestBow Press books may be ordered through booksellers or by contacting:

WestBow Press
A Division of Thomas Nelson
1663 Liberty Drive
Bloomington, IN 47403
www.westbowpress.com
1-(866) 928-1240

Because of the dynamic nature of the Internet, any web addresses or links contained in this book may have changed since publication and may no longer be valid. The views expressed in this work are solely those of the author and do not necessarily reflect the views of the publisher, and the publisher hereby disclaims any responsibility for them.

Any people depicted in stock imagery provided by Thinkstock are models, and such images are being used for illustrative purposes only.

Certain stock imagery © Thinkstock.

ISBN: 978-1-4497-8230-6 (sc)
ISBN: 978-1-4497-8231-3 (hc)
ISBN: 978-1-4497-8229-0(e)

Library of Congress Control Number: 2013900974

Printed in the United States of America

WestBow Press rev. date: 02/04/2013

Author's Note

The story contained in these pages is fiction. I once heard, however, that the most important element in writing fiction is telling the truth. That is what I have attempted to do here. The characters and events in this story are completely fictional, though you can find very similar stories in any jail or rehabilitation center in the country. My purpose in writing this story was partially to entertain but also to put into words the story of thousands of people still searching for the truth.

This story contains scenes that some people might find offensive or shocking. I want to be perfectly clear that these scenes were not included for their shock value, nor are they in any way an endorsement of the activities they portray. They were included in an attempt to illustrate the cold and heartless world inhabited by those living outside the kingdom of God, as well as the desperate measures many of these people will take to find love and acceptance. These are the people most in need of God's saving grace, but sadly, they are the least likely to hear about it. Although the characters in this story are teenagers, it is not really intended for a teenage audience. I believe that parents should exercise their discretion before permitting their children to read this story or any other story.

On the other hand, this is also the story of the saving grace of God, and the miraculous things that happen when one young lady turns her will and her life completely over to doing the work and the will of God. This is a story of the fulfillment of the Great Commission. The Bible tells us that, before he ascended into heaven, Jesus told his disciples to go into the world and make disciples of all men (author's translation). This commission was not limited to "good" people, or just people who are like us. I believe that it was Jesus' intention that we also witness to the drunks, sinners, and tax collectors such as those that Jesus himself witnessed to. There are people in this world—"other people"—who are in desperate need of hearing the gospel but never will unless we make the effort to turn our lives over to his will and truly fulfill the Great Commission.

I hope you enjoy this story, but more important than that, I pray that it will encourage you to become less like the world and more like Jesus Christ. I pray that it will encourage you to go out into the world and try to make disciples of everyone you meet.

John

There was no doubt that John was lost. It had been years since he had been out to his grandfather's farm, and even longer since he had been to the old house there. When his grandfather died, he had left his entire estate, including both houses, to John. That however, had been five years ago. John vaguely remembered how to get to the newer house his grandfather had built near the highway, but that house had been sold a couple of years ago to cover the taxes on the place. Now that he was about to graduate from high school, John was thinking about moving into the old house. First, though, he had to find it. John had not been out to the old house since he was about seven years old, and eleven years can play tricks on a person's memory. To make matters worse, there were a lot of changes that had taken place out this way in just the past couple of years. Where there had once been dairy farms and grain elevators, there were now subdivisions and convenience stores. John didn't really mind the progress, but it did make it just that much harder to find what he was looking for. After nearly an hour of driving down every half-paved road he could find, he pulled into a driveway to ask for directions.

The house at the end of the driveway had once been a nice ranch-style house. It had been several years, however, since anyone had done much in the way of maintenance. The porch was held up in the middle by stacks of cement blocks, and on either end by not much of anything at all. The faded gray paint was peeling off in large pieces. Several windows had been boarded over, and the screen door was leaned against the side of the house. There were Ford tractors and Chevy pickups, and parts for both, scattered everywhere around the place. John was about to leave, thinking that the place was abandoned, when an older man walked out of the door.

John turned off the engine and got out of the car. As he did so, it occurred to him that his appearance was less than comforting. He was dressed in blue jeans and a T-shirt with a black leather motorcycle jacket. His long, straight hair hung loosely around his shoulders, and his eyes were hidden behind a pair of mirrored sunglasses. In the company of his friends, John's appearance was nothing out of the ordinary, but here, he felt obvious. John carefully kept his hands at his sides as he walked up to the house.

"Good morning," he said as he stopped about four feet from the porch where the man stood watching him carefully. As he was just within the shade of the house, John took off his sunglasses so that his face would not be hidden. Even at this distance, John could see the glazed look in the man's eyes and the unsteady grip he had on the rail. He could also smell stale beer, cheap vodka, and pipe tobacco.

"There ain't nothin' good 'bout no morning. There ain't nothin' 'round here worth stealin' neither. Why doncha git back in your car and get on out of here?"

"I was just hoping you could help me out. I was looking for the Snelling house, and I was hoping you could help me find it."

"Wacha wan' there? Sheriff Tate lives there nowadays, an' I don' figure you to be one to go lookin' for the sheriff."

"I'm not lookin' for the sheriff. I'm looking for the old house, the one down by the river. My grandfather left it to me, and I was wanting to check it out before I decide what to do with it."

"You Sharon's boy? You don' much look like 'er."

"Yeah, well I had a father too, and I suppose I look more like him. If you don't mind, just tell me if you know how to get there, and I'll get out of here and leave you alone."

The old man sat down heavily on an old rickety chair that John had failed to notice earlier. He pointed west. "Go on down this road about another half mile or so, and it will be the next road on your left. You ain't gonna see it lessen yer lookin' fer it. There ain't nothin' on that road 'cept for your grandfather's place and some sort of gov'ment land that's been padlocked since the sixties, so they ain't bothered to keep it up much. Ya won' have much luck tryin' to sell the place, though. Most folks 'round here couldn't afford to buy it, and most other folks wouldn't want nothin' this far out. Ya prob'ly stuck with it, though you might be able to rent it out as pastureland."

"Thanks," John said as he put his glasses on and backed his way to his car. "I hadn't really figured on selling though, so I don't think it'll matter too much."

John got into his car, started it up, and backed up onto the road before heading west. The old man hadn't been exaggerating about the road being hard to see. The fence line broke just on either side of the road, where ancient oak trees and dense undergrowth competed to hide the narrow track that headed down the hill. The old road was rutted and unpaved and ran for a couple of miles before the old Victorian home was visible on the left. The gate in front of the driveway stood open, and the driveway itself was in worse condition than the road. John stopped his car just inside the gate rather than risk damaging something, and then he walked up to the house.

The house had stood open to the elements for several years, and the results could be plainly seen long before John even got near the house. The Once-white paint had turned a dull gray where it was still attached to the house. The windows had been boarded up, but some of the boards had fallen off, and the windows in those places were broken out. The front door hung loosely from one hinge, and the porch, which wrapped all the way around the house, sagged in several places. As he got closer, John was struck by the similarities between the house and his grandfather, the man who had built it nearly seventy years before. Both had once stood tall and strong, but in the end were broken down and frail. The difference was that the house looked as though it could be restored to its once-proud stature, where his grandfather was beyond reach.

John stepped carefully across the porch and peered into the dark reaches of the house. There was little light inside, but enough to see that it had not stood completely empty all these years. There were empty bottles laying around and half-charred wood still in the fireplace. He stepped through the door and began looking around. It took several seconds for his eyes to adjust to the dim light. Although it was creaky, the floor inside the house was much sturdier than that of the porch. The inside of the house was in much better condition than the exterior had been. The paint was faded, the wall paper was peeling off, and every corner was thick with cobwebs. Everything seemed sturdy and built to last, though. John wandered through the first floor of the house until he came to the cellar door.

The door was not only still set solidly in its frame, but it was still locked. John reached into his jacket pocket and got out the small ring which held the keys to the house. He tried each in turn until he found the one which unlocked the door. Unlike the rest of the house, there was no light at all in the basement. Since he had not thought to bring a flashlight, he closed the door and relocked it. John finished his investigation of the main floor, and went upstairs. The second floor, like the one below, was completely empty and just as solid. While in one of the rooms where the boards had fallen off the window, John saw a pickup truck bouncing across the field. He went back downstairs and out onto the porch just as the truck stopped at the foot of the stairs.

A big man stepped from the truck. He was a good six inches taller than John and quite a bit heavier. He was also wearing a sheriff's uniform. What little hair he had left was cut short, and he had a full mustache, which was black but streaked with gray. "I got a phone call from Ben Turner saying that there had been a young man stop by his place asking for directions to this place. This is private property, so unless you have a good reason for being here, I suggest that you get back in your car and get out of here."

"Yeah, well this is my private property whether Mr. Turner likes it or not. So, yeah, I would say that I have good reason to be here. I told Mr. Turner as much, and I rather doubt he referred to me as a young man."

"If this is your place, you won't mind giving me your name."

"Not at all. My name is John Overstreet. My grandfather left me this place, and my step-father sold you your house. Now, if you don't mind, I would like to get back to looking around. I will probably be moving out here this summer, and I would like to find out what needs to be done before I do."

"Sorry to bother you then," the sheriff replied, "but we've had some

x

problems with kids bringing their parties and their girlfriends out here, and I was just trying to keep the place from getting any more damaged than it already is. If you have any problems along those lines just give me a call. There's a gate along our fence line, and I can usually get here in about fifteen minutes or so."

Sheriff Blackwell started to get back into his truck. "Oh, one other thing I should tell you. You'd do well to stay away from Ben Turner's place. You're lucky you caught him halfway sober. He has a tendency to shoot people who show up at his house."

"I appreciate the information, but I hadn't really planned on dropping by for a social visit. Since you're here though, now that I'm eighteen and I have a full title to this place, me and my friends are going to be spending quite a bit of time out here. I don't think anybody's going to benefit if we're being stopped and questioned all the time."

"Well, I'd say that if you're going to be out here all the time, then I won't have to. It'll make my job a whole lot easier. Just do me a favor, though. If you're going to be having any parties or anything like that, just let me know in advance what's going on. You're isolated enough out here that I don't think you'll be bothering anyone, but I'd prefer not to have a bunch of teenage drunks driving through the county. The state is really wanting to crack down on that type of thing, and I don't need the hassle."

The sheriff said good-bye, got back in his truck, and drove off across the field. John spent the next hour wandering around the grounds, checking out the other buildings. Other than the barn, they were mostly just piles of firewood. Satisfied for now, John walked back to his car and headed off toward the city. He would need to have an electrician come out and check out the wiring sometime this week, and then have the utilities turned on. Once they had some power and running water, he and his friends could start fixing the place up.

Chris

It had been the longest day Chris had worked in weeks. She did not normally work more than three or four hours a day during the week, but today she had volunteered to work until closing. She was looking forward now to getting home, taking a shower, and going to bed. She did, after all, have to go to school tomorrow. Chris was also planning to go out to John's after school tomorrow for the weekend. As she drove home, her old '75 Dodge had the road to itself. She enjoyed driving late at night. It was always quiet, and there were no little old men to get in her way. It didn't bother her that the car's radio did not work, as it gave her a chance to meditate and reflect.

On this night, she was thinking about graduation and what would come after. Her grades weren't good enough for any kind of scholarship, so if she was going to go to college, it would have to be at the community college which was all she could afford. Between her uncle's disability checks and her mom's paychecks from the 7-Eleven, there was barely enough to pay the bills and put food on the table. There certainly was not enough to pay for tuition.

When she got home, there was a light on in the living room. Her mother was working all night, so it had to be her uncle. Chris had hoped that he would be asleep because she really wasn't up to dealing with him tonight. She walked up the front stairs and unlocked the door as quietly as she could. Inside, she found Uncle Tony asleep on the couch. Passed out would be a better term for it, as there were at least two dozen beer cans scattered around the area where he was snoring loudly. In a glance, Chris took in the pretzel crumbs, spilled beer, and other trash, and she knew she would have to spend at least an hour cleaning it all up before she left for school in the morning. It was just another night at Uncle Tony's house. Chris walked as quietly as she could up the stairs to take a shower.

Chris studied herself in the mirror as she undressed for her shower. At five feet four inches, she wasn't really short, but she wasn't exactly tall either. She considered her face to be quite plain, though aside from a few freckles around the bridge of her nose, her complexion was clear. Although she was slim and fit, there wasn't really anything about her that would stand out. Her reddish-gold hair fell in loose curls around her shoulders. She didn't consider herself ugly, but she didn't think of herself as pretty either; certainly not pretty enough to attract John's attention, which was what she most wanted at this point in her life.

Chris took a quick shower, tossed her dirty clothes down the laundry chute, threw a robe over her shoulders, and went into her bedroom. Although she had been as quiet as she could, she evidently had not been quiet enough. When she walked into her room, Uncle Tony was sitting on her bed, waiting for her and eying her with his usual drunken, lecherous stare. "I've been waiting for you, sweetheart. Why don't you come over here and show your poor Uncle Tony how much you love him?"

Thirty minutes later, Uncle Tony had gone back to his beer, leaving Chris alone with her pain. He had been even more brutal tonight than normal, leaving bruises on her breasts, thighs, and back. Chris cried silently in the dark. She thought about praying, but didn't know who to pray to, or even if there was a God out there who would care about her problems. She swore to herself that she would be moving out of this place as soon as she could and cried herself to sleep. The angels in heaven cried with her.

Chapter 1

After six months of working all weekend, every weekend, the house was nearly ready to move in. After the power had been turned on, John and his friends found that all of his grandparents' furniture had been stored in the basement. Much of it was moldy and had to be thrown out, but some of it was in pretty good condition, enough of it anyway to furnish the house so that it looked livable. There was still much to do, but most of what was left was just cosmetic. There had not been nearly as much work to do as John had originally thought. Most of the serious work they had done involved the porch, driveway, and barn. Nearly all the rest had just been a matter of either patching or painting.

Tonight, John was mostly getting things ready for the big party he was throwing tomorrow. It was the last day of school for seniors in all of the area schools, and John was planning the biggest party in the state. A month ago, John talked to Sheriff Blackwell about the party, and the two of them had come to an agreement. John would lock the gate at ten so that drunks would be kept off the roads, and the sheriff would stay away.

The beer was chilling in the cooler, a root cellar actually that stayed a constant forty-six degrees. There was a small platform set up in the barn for the stereo system, compliments of Ricky, whose father ran a DJ service, and the road had been marked so that everyone could find it. John had even rounded up ten automatic coffee pots for the morning after. All of his friends had gone home to get ready for their last day of school. John would be staying out here for the night and driving into town for school in the morning.

When Chris got home from John's, her mother was just getting ready to leave for work. Her mother was slightly taller than Chris and not quite as slim. Although she kept herself in good shape, her face showed the signs of a stressful life. Chris's father had been a highly successful lawyer with a gambling problem. No one had ever suspected the seriousness of his problem until he put a shotgun in his mouth and put an end to his worries. Even ten years after she had sold everything they owned to pay down the debts, Chris's mom was still trying to pay them off. Chris knew very well where the deep lines and heavy bags on her mother's face had come from. She did the best she could to provide for Chris, but with no education and no training, there just weren't any jobs that paid well enough to make ends meet.

"I'm sorry sweetheart, but I've got to get going. I probably won't get home before you leave for school tomorrow, but I know you'll have a good day; I'm really proud of you. Uncle Tony will be out all night at his poker game, so you'll have the place to yourself tonight." With that, her mother kissed Chris on the cheek and hurried out the door. It was a relief to have one night a week that her Uncle Tony was out playing poker all night. If he wasn't here, he couldn't come visit her late at night. After her mother left, Chris began packing a few things. She and a few others would be spending a week out at John's farm after the party. She would have an entire week without any of Uncle Tony's midnight visits. After that, she hoped to find a place of her own, or at least someplace with a roommate. She really did not have all that much to pack, because she really didn't have all that much to begin with. Chris had at least enough for the week though, and that was all she was really concerned about.

When she finally went to bed, Chris found that she couldn't sleep. The reason of course was simple. She was excited—excited about the last day of school, excited about the party, and excited about getting out from under her uncle's roof. Chris was also anxious because she had decided to tell John how she felt about him, even though she was a little scared about how he would respond.

Unlike most of his friends, Brad couldn't find it in himself to get all worked up over the last day of school. He hadn't really spent enough time there for it to make much of a difference. Right now, the only thing on his mind was the fact that he still did not have a date for the big party. It wasn't that he couldn't find a date—there were plenty of young ladies who would be willing to go with him. It was just that none of them were the one he wanted to take. The more he thought about it, the more Brad had realized that the one girl he was most drawn to was the one least likely to say yes.

Brad had spent the better part of the school year picking on Kate, a girl who sat in front of him in a couple of classes. Kate was everything a good girl was supposed to be and a girl who wanted far more for her life than what Brad had to offer. She was also the prettiest girl Brad knew. At five feet eleven inches, she was the tallest girl in class, with long, dirty-blonde hair, eyes the color of blue ice, and the build of a super model. Even the glasses that she hated so much were perfect for her. Kate was also a Christian. She went to church three times a week, brought her worn Bible with her to school, and mostly talked about her church. Brad, on the other hand, was what some referred to as a freak. His dark-brown hair was longer than most of the girls' in school. He listened to heavy metal music, drank too much, and did not object to taking drugs. It wasn't that Brad didn't believe in Kate's God, but he found it inconvenient. Brad was enjoying his youth, and the church seemed determined to do everything they could to stop him from doing just that.

Despite their differences, Brad found himself thinking about Kate all the time. He had wanted to ask her to the party, but didn't think that she would want to go. After all, tomorrow was Wednesday, and she would most likely be going to church instead. Brad thought about Kate the entire drive home. There were just so many things he didn't know about with Kate. The only thing that was certain was that if he didn't ask her out tomorrow, the last day of school, he most likely would never get the chance again. Even if he didn't ask her to go to the party, he needed to ask her out for another night.

Brad briefly considered asking his mother for advice but quickly discounted the idea. Her bi-polar medication worked wonders when she took it correctly, but that didn't happen very often. The way it usually worked was that she would take a handful at once and be stoned for hours, and then she would feel guilty and not take any more for the next week or so. After about a week, the cycle would start all over. Regardless of where she was on her personal roller coaster, she was very difficult to talk to. It was clear that his mother would be of little help, and none of his friends would be able to understand why he wanted to ask Kate out in the first place. As always, he was on his own.

⁓☙❧⁓

As he sometimes did, Ricky wondered how much his friends would like him if he was not the source for nearly everything. Ricky's father was a pusher, scalper, and a fence, and he used Ricky to sell drugs in the schools. His father's legitimate business was a portable DJ outfit, which he used as a cover for his other activities. If anyone in the school needed a hit, concert tickets, or just about anything else, Ricky was the one they came to. Although his role in his father's business dealings lent him a certain amount of popularity, it wasn't something he liked doing, and he was looking forward to getting out and making an honest living. How many friends would he have then? He was not, he knew, all that likable. There were a few, such as John and Chris and maybe a few others, who would most likely still be around, but he had no way to know for sure. That was why he had worked so hard to get a scholarship out of state. He was certain that if he could just get out of this town and start over somewhere else, his life would finally be his own.

Tomorrow night would be his last fling with his friends. After that, he would be moving on to Colorado. Despite his desperation to get out, Ricky knew that he would miss this town. He had friends here, and friends, however superficial, were not something that he could walk away from casually. Many times he had considered forgetting about leaving, but as much as anything, he wanted to remake his life in a whole new image, and he couldn't do that without changing his geography.

Another thing that was pushing Ricky to move was Chris. She was Ricky's closest friend. Other than John, only Chris knew the what and why of his plans. Although she said that she didn't want him to leave, she understood his situation and was always there to support him as he struggled with the decisions. What made it difficult for Ricky was that he wanted to be much more than friends with Chris, and she knew that as well. The only person she had any interest in though was John, and as much as he wanted to resent that, he knew them both well enough to know she would be better off with John than with him. But he didn't know if he could stay and watch.

Ricky's father was waiting for him when he got home, and it was clear that he wasn't happy. "Where have you been?"

"I was out at John's getting things set up for the party tomorrow. I'm going to make you a small fortune tomorrow night, so just leave me alone."

"You were supposed to be here an hour ago. I needed your help cutting." He punctuated his statement by punching Ricky in the jaw. "What do I need to do to get it through your head that business comes before hanging out with your friends?" He punched Ricky again.

Ricky was not a small person. At six feet four inches and barrel-chested, he was the biggest person in his class, but he was nowhere near as big as his father. He knew from experience that he was no match for his father, and he would stop hitting sooner if Ricky just stood there and took it like the man his father expected him to be. When it was all over, there were no broken bones or obvious bruises; there never were. His father knew how to instill discipline without bothering the good folks at family services. Very soon, Ricky reminded himself, he would be out of here forever, and he would never have to deal with his father again.

April couldn't help but feel guilty. She had never really felt comfortable lying to her parents, even by omission. Unlike most of her friends, April never drank a whole lot and had gotten high only a few times. Her parents would never understand those things, and more than anything else she did not want to disappoint them. They probably had a good idea what would be happening over the next week. They knew that she was going to a party and that there would be drinking going on. They also knew that she would be spending the week with her friends, who were not known for their moderation, out at

John's place. They trusted her judgment, however, and it was that trust that she did not want to betray.

What April's parents did not know was the extent of the partying that would be going on. It was this omission that most bothered her conscience. Despite those guilty feelings, she would be going to the party, and she would be spending the week with John and the rest of the gang. Her parents knew her friends, and they knew how to get in touch with her. She thought that they were being very generous in allowing her to go, though some of her friends thought that they were too strict. Both of her parents lived at home, and they both loved her very much—and April didn't want any of that to change. Most of her friends lived either with one parent or with step-parents. John's father had died when he was a baby; after that, he lived with his step-father and his mother until she passed away just a few years ago. Although April sometimes resented her parents' rules, she always abided by them. She knew exactly how lucky she was.

April was a pretty girl with short, straight brown hair, a Mediterranean complexion, and deep-blue eyes. She was a little on the heavy side, but by no means fat, though she thought she was. She always dressed carefully so that her size wasn't obvious. Officially, she had a boyfriend, Lee, who she had been dating for about a year and a half. Anymore though, the two of them did little more than show up and leave in the same car. April was pretty sure that there was supposed to be more to a relationship than that, but a boyfriend in name only was better than no boyfriend at all, wasn't it? It wasn't as though she got a lot of other offers, and anything was better than being alone.

Her parents were still awake when Lee dropped her off at home, though they were on their way to bed. "We're glad you made it home before we fell asleep, princess," her father told her. "We'll probably be gone by the time you get up in the morning, and we wanted to be sure to tell you to have a good day tomorrow."

"Thanks, Dad," April replied, "but you knew I was going to be home, curfew is just ten minutes from now."

"Will you be here when we get home from work?" her mom asked.

"Yeah, I'll be here. The party doesn't start until eight. There are a bunch of things going on tomorrow afternoon, but I'm just going to wait for the party. Chris might be here. She's going to come over and get ready with me."

"That would be great," her mom told her. "We haven't seen Chris for a while. We'll see you tomorrow then. Good night."

"Good night, Mom. I love you," April said as her parents disappeared up the stairs. April grabbed a soda out of the refrigerator, went upstairs to take a shower, and went to bed. She was looking forward to a good day tomorrow.

※

Shannon had not had much to do with getting things ready for the party. In fact, the only one from the group that she really knew was John, who she met when she started working at the print shop. John, being the kind of guy he was, had immediately invited her to the party when he found out that she was also graduating. To be honest, Shannon was not really sure what to make of John. To some extent, he frightened her. With his long hair and the leather jacket he always wore, he looked a lot like the thugs who were always hanging around her neighborhood. As she had gotten to know him a little better, she began to realize that his appearance was the only thing he had in common with the corner hoodlums. He still made her nervous, though.

In spite of this, Shannon was going to the party. She was honest enough with herself that she knew that her main reason for wanting to go to the party was that she was curious. Most of the white people she knew were either pushers or prostitutes. The rest were teachers and cops. This party would be her first opportunity to get to know a white person on a personal level.

Shannon lived in a black neighborhood and went to a mostly black school. She had never had the opportunity to travel any farther than the downtown mall. Living in a black world, most of what she knew about the rest of the world came from school and television. Shannon also did not see much opportunity in the future for it to be any different. Her parents couldn't afford to send her to college, and she was pretty much tied to the family business. This neighborhood was her world now and in the immediate future. She was, however, intensely curious about what went on outside the monochrome world she lived in.

For Shannon, this party was an opportunity to explore the real white world. It was a chance for her to see for herself if there really was a difference in the way white and black people lived. The idea that a bunch of white kids from the "sticks" might be closet Klansmen made her slightly nervous, but she refused to let it put her off. She was going to take the chance to do what her mother never had the chance to do.

Even in her own world, Shannon did not really feel like she belonged. She knew that she didn't have much in common with the black women whose pictures were found in her text books. Those pictures usually showed large, very-dark-skinned women dressed in little more than rags. Shannon, on the other hand, was of medium height and athletically built. Her skin tone was more of a light almond rather than a dark chocolate. She had dark eyes and long dark hair, and she wore clothes that were fashionable, even if slightly dated. Shannon was a unique person, and she deeply resented the stereo-typed images so often found in popular media.

It was difficult for Shannon to get to sleep that night. A thousand thoughts and images raced through her brain at a thousand miles per hour. This was not really all that unusual for her though, so she knew what she had to do to get her thoughts under control. She closed her eyes tightly and began to pray. Even if she wasn't completely sure that God was out there listening, prayer gave her a sense of peace and allowed her to organize her thoughts so that they could be laid to rest. Almost before she was finished with her prayer, Shannon was sound asleep.

Chapter 2

Chris was ready for her last day of school. She woke up early as usual and began to prepare for the day ahead. She quickly got dressed and fixed herself a couple of eggs for breakfast. Just before she left, Chris called her best and oldest friend, Lyssa. The phone rang several times before Lyssa answered. "Hello," she said groggily when she finally picked up the phone.

"Hey girl, you planning to sleep all day or what?"

"Oh, hi, Chris. I've got two hours before school starts."

"Yeah, but it usually takes you about three hours to get ready. I was just calling to make sure that you were going to be at the party tonight. I haven't had a chance to talk to you all week."

"Do you really think there's any way I would miss it? I'll be there."

"Great, I'll see you tonight then. I'll be a little late; I have to work this afternoon."

"That's all right; I don't plan on being there before nine or so. You're right though; it's going to take me a while to get ready, so I probably need to get going. I'll talk to you later. Bye."

Chris said good-bye, hung up the phone, and walked out the door. Although she was spoiled, and tended to get on Chris's nerves sometimes, Lyssa was the only friend Chris had left from before her father died. Lyssa often had difficulty focusing her attention on anything other than herself, but when Chris's father killed himself, and she had been forced to move to the other side of town, Lyssa's friendship and support had been a vital link to Chris's sanity. She understood that her other friends did not really care much for Lyssa, but they put up with her because of Chris. Next year though, Lyssa would be going away to USC, and Chris wanted to spend some time with her before she left.

On her way to school, Chris pushed thoughts of Lyssa to the back of her mind. Chris was a morning person and liked to work out some before she got started with the day. She did not, however, like the idea of working out at home or running through her neighborhood. So she always tried to get to school at least an hour early so that she could work out safely. The fact that there was an actual gym that she could use for free was important as well. But after today, she would have to find another place to work out.

As usual for that time of the day, only a few people were around when Chris arrived at the school. The secretaries were there, of course, as were a few of the teachers. The school band was in the music room rehearsing for the afternoon assembly. No one else was in the gym though, which was the way Chris preferred it. She started out in the weight room, but she didn't spend a whole lot of time there. After the weight room, Chris headed out to the track to run a few laps. She didn't bother to count laps; she just ran until she couldn't run anymore, and then she walked two more to cool down. Winded and sweaty, she started to make her way back to the locker room.

As she entered the gym, she vaguely noticed some guys entering from the doors on the far side. There was still a good forty-five minutes or so before school started, which made Chris wonder who they were and why they were there. It was then that she recognized Lyssa's step-brother, Rich. "Hey, Chris," he shouted, "wait up."

"Hey, Rich, what are you doing here? You don't go to school here." Chris didn't actually dislike Rich. There was just something about him that made her very nervous.

Rich quickly closed the distance between them across the gym. "I came by looking for you. Me and my buds are ditching school today and going downtown. I thought maybe you might want to come with us."

"I don't think so, Rich. I'm going to enjoy my last day of school."

"Come on, Chris. The five of us will get a head start on the party tonight."

There was something about the look on his face and the tone of his voice that Chris did not like at all. "I don't think I want to join you. You guys go ahead, and I'll see you tonight." Chris began to back her way toward the locker room.

Rich dashed over to her and grabbed her roughly by the arm. "That ain't going to work," he said. "See, we want to party—we want to party *now*, and we want to party with *you*. You know you want to party with us, so quit playing."

Chris opened her mouth to scream but lost her voice when Rich punched her in the jaw. He hit her several more times—in the face, in the chest, wherever he could reach. Chris tried again to scream but could not force the sound to come out of her mouth. The other three joined in then, hitting her and pulling at her clothes. It didn't take long before she had no more fight left in her, and they began to take their turns with her. Rich took his turn first, and then a guy who sort of resembled Sting. A third was just taking off his belt when the school security guard entered the gym.

Chris would never be able to recall anything specific that happened after that. Her mind blanked out, and she slipped into a peaceful world where all the pain went away. Her mind was filled with vague images of a sea of faces crowding around her— some angry, some solicitous, and some just there. The next time that Chris was truly aware of where she was and what was happening, she was lying on an emergency room table. Her clothes, mostly ripped, were sitting on a table nearby, and she had only a sheet to cover her.

John was tired. He had been late getting to bed and had to get up early to make the long drive into town. He definitely was not in the mood to deal with the chaos he ran into at the school. In addition to the usual mess of double-parked cars, there were also a half-dozen police cars and an ambulance. A huge crowd had gathered at the back of the school, near the gym. John parked his car and walked that way, as curious as anyone else as to what was drawing the crowd. Half-way there, he ran into Ricky coming the other way.

"Hey, Rick, what's going on back there?"

Ricky looked at him with fire in his eyes and jerked his head toward the front entrance. "Come on," he said, "I'll tell you about it inside. You don't want to go back there."

John silently followed Ricky until they got inside the main hall of the school. There were far fewer students hanging around the main entrance than usual, as most were rubbernecking outside the gym. Once inside, Ricky pointed to the bench by the office. "You better sit down." Once John was seated, Ricky began to relate the morning's events—at least as Ricky understood them—as he paced back and forth. As the story unfolded, Ricky didn't see John's fists clench or the dark shadow that passed over his face. "Rich had just better hope that he never gets out of prison, 'cause, if he does, I'm gonna kill him."

When Ricky at last finished the story, the two of them stared gravely at each other. There was no reason for them to talk. Each understood very well the shock and rage that the other felt; there just were no words to adequately express it.

Neither moved for several minutes until Principal Derringer, a couple of police officers, and the security guard walked by, returning from the gym. Derringer was about to enter the office when he instead stopped, said something quietly to the officers, and then walked over to where John and Ricky were. "Mr. Overstreet, Mr. Sheldon, I'd like to talk to the two of you. If you would like to wait in my office for a few minutes, I'll be there just as soon as I deal with a few legal issues." He didn't wait for a response but walked through the glass office door and headed to the conference room.

John and Ricky hesitated, wondering if they were going to somehow get blamed for this. When they entered the office, the secretary directed them to the principal's office, where they sat quietly until Principal Derringer entered about fifteen minutes later. When he sat down, John noticed a haunted look on his face that had never been there before. His back was straight, and his shoulders were tense, and a sense of weariness and urgency was apparent in his every action.

"I'm assuming that the two of you have heard what transpired in our gym this morning." Derringer paused a few seconds to allow Ricky and John a chance to respond, which he didn't really expect. "I know that both of you are very close with Ms. Johansson, so I'm going to ask for a favor. I have to accept responsibility for the events of this morning, which means that I also have to accept responsibility for making sure that Ms. Johansson is taken care of. There are 2,500 other students who will be affected by these events. What

I'm asking you to do for me is to go to the hospital and keep me posted on what is happening. I would like you both to come back before the end of the day, but there won't be any consequences against you if you don't."

"We appreciate that, Mr. Derringer," John said. "We'll definitely keep you posted. This isn't your fault, though. There are only four guys who are responsible, and they better hope they stay locked up."

"Gentlemen, I know that we have had more confrontations than conversations over the past four years," Mr. Derringer said, "but I want you to know that I'm not your enemy. If you need someone to talk to, you know where to find me."

Both nodded their heads as they got up to leave the office, but neither said a word until they were halfway to the hospital. Finally, Ricky broke the silence, asking a question that had been burning through his mind all morning. "John, why do you think these things happen to Chris?"

"I don't know, Rick. She does seem to attract more than her fair share of trouble. Maybe Rich figured that she would just be quiet and not say anything. He's probably right too. If they hadn't been caught, probably no one would have ever found out."

"Do you really think that the man is going to do anything to Rich? I mean, his dad's a defense lawyer and his mom's an assistant DA. How many times has he gotten in trouble and not even ended up in court?"

"Yeah, but if they really want to keep him safe this time, they'll lock him up for good. If they don't, and I get my hands on him, he'll die very slowly."

"You're gonna have to take a number, 'cause I get first crack at breaking his head." Nothing more was said, and silence returned for the rest of the trip to the hospital.

It wasn't supposed to be like this, April thought to herself. This was supposed to be the best day of her life, but instead, one of her best friends was lying in an emergency room, victimized by someone who was supposed to be her friend. The brightly colored posters which had been hung up all over the school were pleasant to look at yesterday, but today they seemed tacky and in very poor taste. More than a few had been torn down and now littered the hallway. A day that was supposed to have been filled with excitement and anticipation was instead filled with chaos, despair, and confusion.

About halfway through the morning, all of the seniors were called to the auditorium. There, the normally boisterous class of 1984 sat quietly. Once all the seniors, with a few notable exceptions, were seated, Principal Derringer got up on stage and said a few subdued words. "I know that you all have been affected by the events of this morning. This is not the way any of us wanted to spend this day, but here we are, and I think that it would be best to address the situation directly. One of our own was brutally assaulted right here on this property, and unless we want that event to mar our memories of the last four years, we need to deal with it now. For that reason I have asked Dr. Sarah Phillips, a psychologist who specializes in victims issues, to come and talk to you today. So, if you could lend her your attention for a while, I'm confident that she will have information that will help you through this. … Dr. Phillips."

Dr. Phillips proved to be a rail-thin, middle-aged woman with graying hair, large glasses, and a sharp New England accent. She spoke for about forty-five minutes about the effects of rape on the victim and the victim's friends and family. She also spoke of the need to deal with the effects of such brutality directly and how to avoid the tendency to blame the victim. Dr. Phillips concluded by letting it be known that she would be on the premises for the rest of the day and encouraging anyone who felt the need to come by and talk. April desperately wanted to talk with someone, but she was more intimidated by this well-dressed professional than she was of the emotional storm in her head.

Brad had no idea what was going on at the school across town where most of his friends were attempting to deal with tragedy. He wasn't all that aware of what was going on around him. The only thing that seemed to penetrate his consciousness was the fact that he had one last chance to ask Kate out, and the idea terrified him. He had never been afraid to ask someone out before, but he had never before been as concerned about the idea that she might say no. During the lunch period, he worked up his courage, swallowed his doubts, and sat down at the table across from her.

"Hey, Kate. How's your lunch?" he asked, more for something to say than out of any real concern about the food.

"About the same as always," she replied. "Aren't you going to eat?"

"No, I'm not really all that hungry. In fact, I don't ever plan on being that hungry again. I do have a question for you, though, that doesn't have anything to do with meat substitute patties. I was wondering if you might want to go out with me sometime."

Kate put the fork-full of carrots she had been about to eat back on her plate and looked at Brad for a few moments, her face unreadable. "I didn't think you were ever going to say anything," she said. "Of course I'll go out with you, you fool. I've been trying to get you to ask me out all year. What'd you have in mind?"

"Well, I was sort of hoping you'd go with me to the party tonight, but I wasn't sure you'd be interested." Brad felt as though a large lead ball had been removed from his stomach. "If not, maybe we could catch a movie or something Friday."

"Actually, I had thought about going to that party tonight. I don't know that I'll want to stay very long, but I've never done anything like that before. It is graduation, after all. What time do you want to pick me up?"

Brad couldn't believe what he was hearing. "Well, the party starts at eight, but I thought we could get something to eat first. How does six sound?"

"Six is perfect. Do you know where I live?"

"All I know is that you live out by the lake."

"Well, if you want to take me home after school, I could show you how to get there."

"You're on. I'll meet you by the west door after seventh period. I need to go make a phone call, so I'll catch up to you in English. Bye."

Brad got up and walked out to the pay phone in the hall outside the cafeteria. As he was walking out the door, he literally ran into Lyssa.

"Hey Brad, are you ready for tonight?"

"I've been ready for tonight for at least three months now. Are you going?" Brad asked, hoping the answer would be no.

"Of course I'm going. I wouldn't miss this for anything. What were you and Kate talking about?"

"I'm taking Kate to the party tonight. We were just making plans."

"Yeah, right. Kate's going to the party, and you're taking her? I wouldn't put money on either one of those happening in this universe."

"I don't suppose you have to believe, but she's going, and I'm taking her. Now, if you'll excuse me, I need to make a phone call." Brad had learned a long time ago that if he kept his conversations with Lyssa short and polite, he was much less likely to cuss her out.

After sitting in the emergency room for nearly three hours with no word, John and Ricky were beginning to worry more than a little. They saw Chris's mom come through about a half hour after they got here, but she didn't say anything to them, and they hadn't seen her since. Finally, a nurse in a crisp, white uniform came out and walked over to where they were sitting. "Are you the two young men waiting on word about Ms. Johansson?"

"Yes, we are," they both said together. "How's she doing?"

"We're about to release her, and her mother's going to take her home. She's okay physically, but not so much emotionally. A few bruises are the extent of her injuries, but she's been through a very traumatic situation. It'll be a long time before she's anywhere near 'fine' again. You and anyone else she's going to be around are going to have to be very careful. Chris is in a very fragile state right now, and she will be for some time to come."

"Can we see her now?" John asked.

"I'm afraid not. Her mother is with her right now, and she's pretty adamant that there won't be any visitors."

"Do you have a phone we could use, then? We told Principal Derringer that we would call when we had news."

"You can use the phone at the desk. You know, Chris is very lucky to have friends who care enough to sit here for hours for her. She's really going to need that friendship and support, maybe for years." Without another word, the nurse turned and walked back through the door into the emergency room.

Back in the treatment area, the nurse went directly to the room where Chris was waiting for her mother to finish the paper work so she could go home. Once there, she found Chris alone putting on the clothes her mother had brought from home. She didn't know where the mother had gone but figured that she hadn't gone very far. "Are you ready to go, hon?" the nurse asked.

"I guess so, but I hurt all over," Chris answered.

"The bruises should all go away in a few days, but there are other pains that won't disappear so easily. Do you have that number for the Rape Hotline I gave you?"

"Yeah, I got it. Thank you for everything you've done."

"Sweetheart, I haven't done nearly enough. I wish there was more I could do, but there isn't. Probably, the best place for you to find help is from your friends. There were a couple of young men who have been outside waiting on you all morning. I think they may have left now; I don't know. If they care about you as much as they seem to, they'll be a much bigger help than I could be. Do you have a boyfriend?"

"No. There's a guy I wish was my boyfriend, but I doubt he'll want anything to do with me now."

"Oh, hon, what those creeps did to you has not changed anything about who you are. If that boy liked you before, then there's no reason he wouldn't like you now."

The nurse was about to say something else, but just then Chris's mother walked back into the room. "Let's go," was all she said before turning and walking back out. Chris followed, bringing an end to the conversation.

As Chris was getting into her mother's car, she saw John's car pulling out of the parking lot. So John had been one of the boys who had been waiting for her. She knew that it had been her mother who had refused to allow her to have any visitors. Chris also knew that her mother was as angry as she had ever seen her, but she didn't know why. In fact, her mother had said very little since she had arrived at the hospital and was now driving in complete silence. It wasn't until they got home that her mother spoke again.

"You stupid little tramp," her mother said, unable to be silent any longer. "If you hadn't gone and flashed that hot little body of yours all over town, this would never have happened."

"I didn't do anything, Mom."

"You're nothing but a little whore, and those boys know it as well as everyone else. It wasn't enough that you sucked your uncle into your sick little world; now you've gone and dragged me into this mess. I'm tired of dealing with all your baggage, and I want you out of here. Just pack your bags, get out, and don't come back. I have to go back to work, and when I get here tonight, I expect your room to be empty." With that, her mother stormed out of the house, and Chris collapsed on the couch in tears. So her mother knew about Uncle Tony; she had always known, and she blamed Chris.

After several teary minutes, Chris went upstairs to take a shower. She was dirty. She could still feel those hands all over her at once. She scrubbed every part of her body several times, seeming to forget that she had just washed there. She scrubbed herself over and over again until she ran out of hot water. When Chris stepped out of the shower, she hurriedly threw her clothes on even before she had completely dried off. She went into her room and stuffed as much as she could into her bags and took them downstairs. She didn't know how she was supposed to go anywhere; her car was still at the school.

When she got to the bottom of the stairs, she found her uncle sitting in his chair staring out the window. "Chris," he said, still not looking at her, "I need to talk to you."

Chris wanted to keep walking, but there was something in his voice she had never heard before, and she didn't know what it was. Compelled, she put her bags by the door and went into the living room to see what he wanted. She was fully prepared to kick him if she had too; she was done with that.

"When your mom called and told me what happened this morning, I was furious," he said, though he still hadn't moved. "I wanted to murder those boys, but then it dawned on me that what they did to you was no worse than what I've been doing to you for years." He fell silent for a few moments, and Chris saw what looked like tears welling up in his eyes from his reflection in the window. "What I've done is a lot worse though, because you should have been able to trust you mother's brother to not hurt you like that. I know that I can't change what I've done, but I wish I could. If it's any help, I'm sorry." Finally, he turned to look at her. When he did, there was no sign of the lust that was usually there. "I don't expect you to forgive me, but I wanted you to know that I love you, and I'll never bother you again. I stopped by the school and picked up your car. It's outside in the driveway."

Chris didn't trust herself to respond, so she turned around, grabbed her bags, and left her uncle's house forever.

When they left the hospital, John and Ricky went back to school. Neither of them was really in the mood to sit and listen to lectures about the Vietnam War, the square roots of imaginary numbers, the conjugation of verbs, or whatever teachers talked about on the last day of school, but they felt that they needed to go back and let some people know what was going on. John parked his car and looked at the building. He had never really cared very much about school, but never before had it stirred in him anything like the hatred he now felt for the building.

"I've been thinking," John said. "Maybe it would be better if I just canceled the party tonight."

"I've thought about that too, but I don't know that we can at this point. There are people coming from all over the place, and there's no way we could get the word out to everyone that it's canceled. Besides, even though I don't feel much like celebrating, I could sure use several stiff drinks."

"You're probably right. If we're going to go through with this, though, don't think you can skip out on me. I'm gonna need you, dude."

"You know you can count on me. What are we going to do with Chris? You know she's not going to want to stay at her uncle's, and a big party probably wouldn't be any better."

"We'll think of something. We need to let April know what's going on, and I'm sure that a lot of other people are going to have questions as well."

They got out of the car and walked up to the school. The first thing they did was to check in at the office where they found Principal Derringer waiting for them. Derringer didn't say anything; he simply shook their hands and went back to lock himself in his office. "This whole ordeal has him pretty torn up," one of the secretaries told them. "He hasn't talked to anyone since you two left this morning, and he only came out of his office once to send his resignation to district. These things aren't supposed to happen at school."

"He's a good man," Ricky told her. "I never really appreciated that before today. He shouldn't be blaming himself."

Coming out of the office, they saw Chris entering the front door of the school. "Chris," Ricky said, "what are you doing here? I figured you'd be at home, which is where you need to be."

"I need to get the rest of my stuff," she told them. "Besides, I don't have anywhere else to go. My mom kicked me out."

"What?" John asked. "Why would your mom kick you out? On second thought, I don't think I want to know." He dug his house key out of his pocket. "Here, go on out to my house and get some rest. We'll get your things and see you when we get there."

"Thanks guys," Chris said. "I still have to stop by work and let them know that I'm taking a sick day, but I'll be there by the time you get home. First, I need to get some things taken care of in the office, and then I'm out of here."

Every word Chris spoke felt like another lead weight hanging from John's heart. Her voice was as dead as her eyes. Every thing about her told John that the vibrant girl he had known for years was lost. It took every ounce of energy he could muster to keep himself from giving in to the rage he felt, afraid it would only make things worse. Once they were down at the other end of the hall, well out of earshot, Ricky gave voice to how he felt. "I don't care if they send Rich to prison or not, I'm gonna kill him."

Once she was inside the office and out of John and Ricky's line of sight, Chris couldn't hold the flood of tears back any longer, and she began crying like a baby. Before anybody even realized what was happening, Principal Derringer had his hands on her shoulders and was gently guiding her to one of the benches that lined the wall. When she saw who was touching her, she involuntarily jerked away from his touch, curled up on the bench, and wept even harder. Mr. Derringer's hands brought painful flashes of the morning, even as she was overcome with guilt by the injured look on his face.

After about ten minutes, the tears subsided, and Chris was able to take care of her business. She awkwardly apologized to Mr. Derringer and practically ran from the place that only this morning she had considered a safe haven. She got back in the car and drove to Carter's where she worked as a hostess. By the time she got there, she had composed herself enough that she felt nearly normal, but only because she couldn't see herself.

Chris entered through the back door and found Joe, the owner, in his office. It was a small office, barely large enough for the hulking mass of a man who occupied it, much less the mixed-matched desk, chairs, and bookshelves that shared it with him. He was on the phone, but when he saw Chris, he immediately excused himself and waved her in as he hung up the phone. Joe's office always made her feel claustrophobic anyway; there was no way she was stepping foot in it today. She stood just outside the doorway. "I wanted to let you know that I'm not going to be able to come in tonight, Joe. I just can't do it today."

"I already figured that, Chris. I was just on the phone setting up getting coverage. I heard about this morning. I didn't even expect you to come by. I want you to take off as much time as you need. I'll clock your hours, and you can consider it paid leave. I don't want you coming back until you're really ready to come back."

"You can't afford that, Joe. I don't need any more than tonight off. I'm already off all next week."

"I'd rather lose that money than risk losing you, Chris. If you can come back after next week, great—I'll see you then. I don't think it's going to work out like that, though. Look, you've been here two years now, and you've done everything I've asked you to. You've volunteered your time to help me out several times, and you're here practically every day. I don't have any kids of my own, and I've grown sort of attached to you. If nothing else, just do it to humor an old man."

"An old fool is more like it, Joe. I'll tell you what: I'll call you next week, and we'll talk about it then."

"I can agree to that. For now, though, I want you to get out of here. I want you to go take care of yourself. We'll all be here when you get back, and I'll be expecting your call."

John and Ricky both went back to their respective classes. When John walked into his history class, April squealed loudly and nearly knocked him down as she ran at him. "How is she, John? Is she going to be okay?"

Mr. Brown, the teacher, said nothing. In fact, Mr. Brown looked like he was trying very hard to not look like he was listening. Meanwhile, John was trying to disentangle himself from April. "She's fine. At least she is physically. She's pretty bruised up, but there's no real damage. I can't say what she might be going through in her head, though."

"Is she at home?"

"No, I guess her mom kicked her out for some reason. Right now she should be on her way out to the farm. I can't say what she's going to do later, though, 'cause I doubt that she's going to want to be at the party."

April was shocked. "You're still going to have the party?"

"I thought about canceling it, but I don't think I can at this point; it's all just too big and too late. Besides, it might be a good thing to let everyone blow off some steam tonight."

April and John walked to where they sat toward the back of the class. "I got a question for you," John said. "Do you think that your parents would let Chris stay with you for a while? I mean, she can stay out at the farm as long as she wants, but after everyone leaves next week, it might be uncomfortable for her to be out there with just me."

"Maybe, but I wouldn't make plans. My parents like Chris, but she makes them uncomfortable, especially my dad. Given the situation, though, they might be talked into it."

"Well, see what you can do. She just doesn't have many options right now."

Chris sat in her car for a long time just staring at the house. She had never been out here by herself before, and didn't really want to be out here now. The big, old house had always given her the creeps, but now it seemed almost menacing. Finally, tired of sitting there being afraid of shadows, she got out of her car and walked up to the house. Once she was inside, it seemed that the house creaked and groaned even more than usual. Chris found herself checking around corners and keeping her back to the walls. Without really even thinking about what she was doing, she found herself on the phone dialing the number John had listed for the sheriff's office.

"Baxter County Sheriff's Office, how may I direct your call?" came a deep, dry male voice on the other end of the line.

"Is Sheriff Blackwell in the office right now?"

"Yes, he is. Can I tell him who's calling?"

"My name is Christine Johansson."

After a few moments, Sheriff Blackwell's familiar, rough voice came on the line. "Sheriff Blackwell, speak your mind."

"Hi Sheriff, this is John's friend, Chris. I don't know if you remember me or not."

"Sure, I remember you. What can I do for you, young lady?"

"Well, this is going to sound sort of silly, but I'm out here at John's by myself right now, and I'd rather not be. I was sort of hoping I could talk you into coming out and just hanging out until John gets here."

"I suppose that I could do that. Let me ask you a question first, though. I'm pretty sure I saw your name come across my desk this morning. Are you the young lady who, uh ... had the problem at school this morning?"

"Yeah, that would be me, which is why I don't like being here alone."

"I'll tell you what; I've got a young deputy named Karen here. What would you say if I brought her along? The two of us can keep you company until John gets there."

Chris's voice was thick with relief. "That would be great. I'll wait for you out on the porch."

She hung up the phone and hurried outside to sit on a bench next to the door. From there she could see everything. Drawing up her feet on the narrow bench, Chris hugged her knees close to her chest and waited quietly for the sheriff.

About fifteen minutes later, Sheriff Blackwell and Deputy Karen Walker pulled up in the driveway. Deputy Walker was young, perhaps a couple of years older than Chris. She was tall and athletic and looked even taller in her uniform. Her Indian ancestry was apparent in her dark-brown eyes, bronzed skin, and long, straight black hair. The three of them sat on the porch making small talk for a while until Chris could no longer feel her heart pound against her rib cage.

As much as Chris wanted to have people around, and as grateful as she was that these two were here, their presence made her more and more uncomfortable. She didn't know if she wanted them to leave or to stay—she just felt guilty about wasting their time. She struggled with it all for a while when Deputy Walker, guessing how she felt, suggested that she go inside and get some rest while the two of them waited for John. Chris thanked them both for coming and for understanding and fled inside the house, which now felt safer to her. She practically ran up the stairs and into the bathroom. While the sheriff and the deputy chatted uncomfortably on the porch, Chris got into the shower and scrubbed herself until her skin was bright red.

When at last the longest school day in history was over, John met a couple of friends in the parking lot to get them updated before getting in his car and heading home. It was a forty-minute drive from the school to the farm, and John used that time to reflect on the day's events. The fact that John had a crush on Chris was not really a secret. He'd had one since the day he met her. Even to this day, six years later, he could still remember how she looked that day. He had gone over to see April, who was his "girlfriend" at the time. When he got there, she was sitting on her front porch with her new next-door neighbor. He could still see the bright green eyes and feathered strawberry-blonde hair that gave her an elfish look. She was wearing faded jeans and a red-and-blue rugby shirt. Beneath the cheerful smile, he could see the grief of losing her father. John knew that she was the prettiest girl he would meet.

He hated the fact that he wasn't able to go out with her then; he was, after all, still going steady with April. After he and April had broken up, he was still uncomfortable asking her out because she was friends with his ex. Later, when he discovered what was going on with her uncle, he had been afraid he would scare her. Now, fate had placed just one more barrier between them, keeping her just beyond his reach.

John was honest enough with himself to understand that a large part of the rage he felt for Rich was selfish. It probably would not have bothered him nearly as much if he wasn't in love with Chris. He had never really thought much about rape before; things like that seemed to happen in other places to other people. Life was supposed to be safer and easier in the Midwest. That had been an illusion that was now gone forever.

When he pulled into his driveway, John saw the sheriff's car parked there, and the sheriff and a deputy on the front porch. He had to struggle hard to fight back the panic that was trying to rise in his chest. He could not imagine what disaster would have Sheriff Blackwell sitting on his front porch.

John parked his car in front of his garage and walked up to the house. "What's up, Sheriff?"

"Nothing, really. Your friend was a little nervous being here alone, so she called and asked if someone could come by and keep her company. Me and Deputy Walker didn't have anything else going on, so we came on over to keep her company. We talked for a little while, but right now she's upstairs lying down. I doubt she's sleeping, but she's at least lying on the bed."

"Thanks for coming by then. I never even thought that she might be bothered by being alone."

"You'll find that there's several things you're going to have to consider where she's concerned that you normally wouldn't," Deputy Walker told him.

"She's a pretty tough young lady, but in situations like this, that may not be a good thing. You're going to have to be very careful about what you say and do around her, but you also need to try not to be too obvious about it."

"I don't know how to do that. I don't know anything about these things. I don't want to know anything about these things. I just want it all to go away."

"It don't matter what you want," said Blackwell, "you're gonna have to deal with what you got, for your own sake as well as hers. Is she gonna be staying out here with you for a while?"

"Well, that's up to her. She's more than welcome to stay as long as she wants, but I don't know that she'll want to stay out here with me. I imagine she'll definitely want to be somewhere else tonight."

"Are you still having that party tonight?"

"I don't know that there's any way to stop it at this point. I thought about having you park one of your deputies at the end of the road, which would definitely send them elsewhere, but then someone's gonna end up drunk in Ben Turner's pasture and get themselves shot. The whole thing has just gotten too big, but I still don't know where Chris can go."

"Why doesn't she just go home?" asked Walker.

"I don't know. Her mom freaked out about something and kicked her out of the house."

Sheriff Blackwell looked pained as he rubbed his forehead. "Well, this may seem inappropriate, but enjoy the party. Just keep our deal in mind. The gate gets locked at ten, and no one leaves here drunk."

"Don't worry; I don't need any more problems either. I'll make sure that everyone stays right here."

"We need to get back to the office, but you know the number if you need anything. You take care of that young lady up there. I would have to take it personally if any thing else happened to her."

They said their good-byes, and John stood on the porch to watch Blackwell and Walker leave before going inside. Sure enough, John found Chris upstairs, lying on a bed and staring up at the ceiling. John had made a point of making noise coming up the stairs, but Chris still jumped when he knocked on the door frame. "Sorry," John said, "I didn't mean to startle you. I just wanted to make sure that you were all right."

"I'm okay, considering. You don't have to stand outside the door. I promise not to try jumping out the window if you come in. It is your room after all."

John stepped just inside the door but stayed there. "We have something of a small problem. I don't want you to think that I'm trying to run you off or anything, but there is no way I can possibly call off the party. I was thinking that you might want to think about finding somewhere else to hide out for the night."

"I don't want you to cancel the party, and I don't want to go anywhere else either. I'm staying right here and getting stoned out of my mind. I know that it won't make things better, but at least for one night I can put everything off to the side and maybe have a little bit of fun despite myself."

"Well, you can certainly stay if you want, but are you sure that's what you really want to do?"

"No, but that's what I'm going to do. Look John, I know that you're trying to look out for me, and I really do appreciate it. The truth, though, is that I don't really see things getting any worse. It's all uphill from here. There is nowhere else I want to be while I'm dealing with this than right here, and no one else I want to be around other than my friends; that's why I keep you all around in the first place." She smiled a little, but John could see that there was no joy in it.

"Whatever you think you should do, that's what you need to do, but don't forget that this room's here and there's a lock on the door. If you start feeling odd at any time, just come on up here and lock the door. Nobody's gonna blame you for hiding out."

Chapter 3

Ricky was having a hard time concentrating on what he was doing. His father had given him very precise instructions on what he was supposed to load for the party. Tonight's party was going to be the biggest bash of the year, and Ricky's father was already making plans for what he was going to do with his profits. His business, Snow White Entertainment, was supplying the night's diversions. The DJ equipment was being supplied at a slight discount, but the drugs were not. In fact, his father had cut the stuff even more than usual and raised the prices. The problem was that Ricky was thinking more about Chris than he was about loading the van. Ricky had to recount everything three times before his count came out right.

By the time the van was loaded, Ricky was running late. He had promised to be at John's by five so that he could help get everything set up, but it was already a quarter till when he backed out of the driveway and headed out of town. "One more time, Dad, and you're going to have to find someone else to be your mule," Ricky said to himself as he drove. Ricky had no intention of ending up like his brother who was doing ten years in the pen because their father sold him out to protect himself. Even though he wouldn't be leaving for school until August, he swore that after he dropped off the van tomorrow, he would never again see or have anything to do with his father.

Thirty minutes later, Ricky pulled up in front of the barn where John was busy setting up tables. "Sorry I'm late, dude. It took me longer than it should have to get the van loaded up."

"Don't worry about it," John told him. "I'm just getting started myself. I just got off the phone with Brad. He'll be here, but won't be able to make it early. Something about some new girl he's bringing."

"Another one? What's that make the total for the year now?"

"I don't know. I lost count after ten. Since he's not going to be here, we might just have to accept that not everything's gonna be the way we want it. Lee and April should be here soon though, and Shannon said she would try to get here early."

"Shannon? Is she that new black girl at the print shop?"

"Yeah, that's her. She said she would try to make it early, but her date might have other ideas. I guess he doesn't really want to come."

"So, where's Chris?"

"I think she's taking another shower. It shouldn't take too long, though. I should be just about out of hot water."

There had to be some sort of mistake. Brad had long ago stopped believing that these things didn't happen to him or his friends, but how could one person attract so many problems? Brad had never gotten too close to Chris. She tended to get a little uptight about some of the ways Brad spent his time, but he did think of her as a friend. In truth, Brad tended to ignore the girls who were not interested in him, and the only person Chris was interested in was John, though John was the only one who couldn't see that.

If Brad was going to take Kate out to dinner before the party, he needed to get moving. Somehow, though, he couldn't bring himself to get motivated. Brad knew a lot of people who moved, to various extents, on the other side of the law, but somehow rape had never come up before. He would never have guessed how shocking it could be when it did.

Even though he was concerned about Chris and how she had been horribly violated, Brad was most concerned about John. Life had been tough on Chris, but that had forced her to grow emotionally stronger than most people would ever give her credit for. He was pretty sure that she would cope and come out the other end alive and well. John, on the other hand, tended to come across as a tough guy, but Brad knew that was just an act. The reality was that John was a very open and friendly guy, and he tended to get emotionally wrapped up in the people he called friends. In the case of Chris, John was so firmly fixated on her that this might very well tear his world apart.

Brad also had a reputation for being cold and heartless. But Brad was one of those rare individuals who were able to detach themselves from their emotions and consider things logically. He was, in fact, very well aware of his feelings. More importantly, he was always aware of the emotions of those around him and how they were affected by those emotions. He considered how these events would affect the people around him. Chris was a survivor. Despite being the victim, she just might make it through better than most others. April would be devastated; she was the most emotional. Lee might not even notice. Ricky was the most likely to react violently. He was pretty angry with the world in general anyway. Even Lyssa would be affected, but she was so self-absorbed it was hard to say how much. John's reaction was the hardest to figure. John tended to suppress his anger, but he had a very long fuse and an explosive temper.

It was almost six when Brad realized how late he was running. He had been sitting in the same place for nearly an hour since he got off the phone with John. He decided that he should call Kate and let her know that he would be late.

"Hi Kate," he said when she answered the phone, "this is Brad. I just wanted to let you know that I was going to be running a little late."

"That's fine. I'm a little behind myself. What's up?"

"I just got a little distracted. I'll tell you about it later. I should be by in about a half hour or so."

"I'll be here waiting. You realize, of course, that means you're going to have to meet my father. He can be a little overprotective at times."

"Well, it's not my favorite thing, but I think I can deal with it. I'll see you soon, bye."

Brad hung up the phone and began rushing around the house to get ready. He had never been late for a date before. Man, what a messed-up day this turned out to be. Too bad life didn't have a reset button.

Chapter 4

Shannon had known about the party for several months. She hadn't originally intended to go, until she started working in the print shop and met John. It was then that she had changed her mind. Her boyfriend, Isaac, still didn't want to go, saying it was just going to be another "straight vanilla" party. Shannon and Isaac had been having problems recently, and it was her hope that going out together to someplace different, like this party, might help out their relationship. Shannon had told John that she would try to show up early and that the two of them could help set up. Isaac had not shown up until the last minute, however, so the party was already started by the time they got there.

"I don't know why you wanted to come to this thing," Isaac said. "It ain't gonna' be nothing but a bunch of white kids getting drunk. Me and you are really going to stick out against all the rednecks."

Shannon swallowed a sigh; they had already been through this conversation. "I told you, John is my friend, and he invited us. Besides, I thought it might be nice to get out and do something for a change rather than hanging out in the street like we always do. If you give it a chance, you might actually have a good time."

"I doubt it. I'm just letting you know, if I'm the only black guy here, I'm gone."

As Isaac pulled into the yard just after eight-thirty, Shannon was surprised to find that there were already a bunch of cars packed in. There wasn't very much room left to park. Isaac finally found a spot, and the two of them began walking toward the barn where most of the activity seemed to be taking place.

Shannon reached out to try to hold his hand, but he ignored her. He walked in front, staying at least two paces ahead of her.

Inside the barn, Shannon was relieved to see other black kids there—not many, but there were some. Although she had insisted that they would be there, she hadn't really been sure. Isaac stood just inside the door looking around. He still wasn't smiling, but at least he didn't look angry anymore.

"There's a few brothers here," he said to her. "Maybe this won't be so bad after all."

"Let's just try to have some fun tonight, okay?" Shannon replied. "There's John over by the tables. I want you to meet him."

The two of them walked over to where John was standing, talking to a small group. As they crossed the room, Shannon, always curious about what was going on around her, listened to bits and pieces of conversations. Most of them concerned something that had happened at school that morning. Nobody was saying who did what, only that it was bad. A few seemed angry, a couple seemed to think it was funny, but most simply agreed that it was a terrible story. As they got closer to where John was, she began to pick up bits of what he was saying.

"I don't know what to do," John was saying. "I would really like to beat on his head for an hour or two, but the cops have tucked him away safely. It wouldn't change what happened anyway."

"John," Shannon said as they got to within a few feet, "I want you to meet my boyfriend, Isaac."

"Hi Shannon," John said as he extended his hand to Isaac. "It's good to meet you, Isaac. Shannon talks a lot about you."

"Don't believe everything she says," Isaac said. "I'm not really that bad."

John laughed. "I'll keep that in mind. Why don't the two of you get yourselves something to drink, or if you're looking for something stronger, you'll have to talk to Ricky over by the sound system. You can put in any music requests you have at the same time. He's got just about everything."

"Do you mean everything in the way of music," Isaac asked, "or drugs?"

"Both," John replied.

"Why don't you go on over, Isaac?" Shannon said. "I'll be there in a bit. I want to talk to John for a minute."

After Isaac had gone off toward where Ricky was doing business, Shannon turned to John. "What's going on, John? People all over the place are talking about something happening today. Then I get over here, and you're talking about beating somebody."

"I'm sorry, Shannon. I don't want to be rude, but I've been trying all night to get away from this conversation. Let's just say that Chris had a rough morning and leave it at that for now."

"Sorry, John. I guess I was being a little nosey. I'll talk to you later. I'd better catch up to Isaac. God only knows what he's buying." Shannon moved off into the crowd as John walked toward the door.

Shannon had met Ricky a few times. He often came into the print shop where she worked, either to talk to John or to pick up flyers for his father's business. She had talked with him a couple of times, but she was not real sure what she thought of him. Shannon knew that the family business included much more than just sound systems, and, although she sometimes used, she had never met a pusher that was worth an ounce of spit. There was something about Ricky, though, that set him apart from other pushers she'd met. As she walked over to where Isaac and Ricky were doing business, they both looked up at her, and Shannon suddenly understood what that something was that she had noticed about Ricky. It was his eyes. The eyes of most people who dealt drugs were either dead or glazed over like Isaac's. Ricky's eyes, however, had fire in them, or maybe passion would be a better word. There was a passion there that she didn't understand.

When she got up next to Isaac, Shannon wrapped her arms around his chest. "Hey there lover, what ya got?"

Isaac handed Ricky some cash, put one of the joints he had just bought in his mouth, and lit it. "Just a little something to make the evening go better." Isaac handed her the joint, which she accepted, and began to lead her back toward the doors.

Kate knew that it had been a mistake to agree to go to this party tonight. She had never been to a party like this one before, and it had sounded sort of exciting earlier today. However, as Brad's van turned off the highway onto a seemingly random county road, she was scared. She was even more scared, though, of admitting to Brad that she was having second thoughts. Kate had wanted to go out with Brad ever since she first met him, and she couldn't bring herself now to tell him that she wanted to go home.

"Where's this place at?" she asked.

"It's down by the river," Brad told her. "I promise that I'm not just taking you out to the country to get lost and run out of gas on some dark road."

"I'm going to hold you to that." Kate laughed. "I was just asking because I've never been out this way before. I never even knew this area was out here."

"Neither did I until about six months ago. That's when John turned eighteen and moved out here. We started coming out here to help him fix it up."

"You mean that he moved out here while he was still in school?"

"Yeah, it's been just him and his step-father for a while. Although they get along okay, they were both ready for John to move out."

"What about his parents?"

"They're both dead. His dad caught the attention of a sniper in Vietnam, and his mom died in a car crash about three years ago. It's just been him and Bill since then. It's been a weird situation, and they were both happy to be done with it."

Kate thought quietly about what Brad said. It often seemed as though Brad could be two different people. Most of the time he was cocky, arrogant, and charming, and he didn't seem to be concerned with much other than himself. At other times, though, Kate could see that there was much more to him than he was willing to admit to. When he had come by to pick her up, he had spent several minutes talking alone with her father, and they evidently got along pretty well. Then, over dinner, he had talked to her about a lot of things he had never talked much about in school. She had heard him say some unexpected things—things that were caring, sensitive, and compassionate.

Now there was the comment about his best friend's parents—a comment that seemed both cold and compassionate at the same time.

"You never told me what came up that had you running late," Kate said.

"Yeah, I guess I should before we get out to the farm," Brad said. "When we get out there, don't be surprised if everyone is a little moody. One of our friends, Chris, was raped this morning before school."

"Oh no," Kate said. "Did they catch the guy who did it?"

"Yeah, caught him in the act. The idiot and his friends attacked her in the school gym."

"Did she know the guy?"

"You better believe it. So do you for that matter. That would be why Rich Perry wasn't in school today. Anyway, Chris is sort of special, so there are going to be quite a few people who will be upset about it. It's really going to bother John, who's had a crush on her for years. So, you might want to be careful about what you say."

"I can imagine. What about the girl—is she all right?"

"About as well as possible I guess. I'm going to try to talk to her tonight. I imagine she'll be hiding out in the house."

"Why doesn't she just go home?"

"*That* is a long story, and one I don't really understand all that well."

"I've never really liked Rich very much, but I never thought that he would do something like that."

"Then you don't really know him. This isn't the first time he's done this; it's just the first time he's been caught. He's nothing more than a spoiled rich boy who thinks he's entitled to whatever he wants. Since his mother is the assistant prosecuting attorney, and his step-father is a defense lawyer, he's under the impression that the system won't touch him."

The rest of the trip passed in silence as Kate contemplated the cruel fate of people she didn't know, and Brad was trying to convince himself that it was anger that he was suppressing.

Chris stood by one of the upstairs windows and looked out at the party spilling out from the barn below; she was watching for Lyssa's car. Part of her wanted to go down to the party, find the biggest bottle of whatever was there, and drown her problems. She knew, though, that it wouldn't help much. She had already drunk quite a bit, and although it made her head feel fuzzy, it hadn't helped her forget. Still, she was already unsteady on her feet, and it really wouldn't take much to knock her out. Then at last, this whole, miserable, rotten day would finally be over.

Below her, she could see John walking around the yard, talking to people. Chris wondered what he thought of everything that had happened. Even though she shuddered at the thought of being touched, Chris wanted more than anything for John to come up here and hold her in his arms. Most likely, though, Chris figured that John wouldn't want anything to do with her. Who would want her now? Would anyone ever be able to see past what happened? Everyone would know, and many would think that she had asked for it. Would John think that about her? Her mother obviously did. Today was supposed to be the day that would mark the change in her life. Everything was supposed to be different now, better. Instead, everything was just the same, maybe worse, than it had always been. Maybe she should follow Ricky's plan and just go away someplace far distant from all the pain and misery here. Could she really go away without knowing for sure how John felt about her? Did she really want to know?

Chris wrapped her arms around her chest. Her skin was dry and chapped from all the soap, and still she felt as though she needed another shower. Maybe if her skin was really dried out, no one would want so desperately to touch her again. Maybe if she put on a few more pounds, guys wouldn't look at her that way anymore. Then again, maybe not. These same thoughts had been going through her head all day, and she still didn't have any answers. Maybe there weren't any answers, and this was what she would have to put up with for the rest of her life. If so, Chris knew it wouldn't be long before she went crazy.

Her thoughts were interrupted by a knock on the door. "Come on in," she said.

When the door opened, it was April and Lee. "Hi, Chris. How are you holding up?" April asked.

"Honestly? Not so good."

April walked over to her and started to give her a hug but stopped short of touching her. Instead, she just looked at her with her heart in her eyes. "I wish there was something I could do. I really want to help."

"I don't know what you could do, April," Chris said. She was grateful that April had not tried to wrap her up in one of those great hugs she was famous for, yet desperately wishing that she would. "You could stay here and keep me company for a while. I've had enough of being alone. I really need someone to talk to."

"Do you want me to leave?" Lee asked from the doorway.

Chris looked over to where Lee was standing, looking as though he were afraid to come close to her, which he probably was. "No Lee, I don't want you to leave, but if you would rather go back to the party, I don't want you to feel like you have to stay either. You can come in if you want."

Lee entered the room but moved to the chair in the far corner of the room. "I wasn't really having a very good time anyway. The whole day is pretty much down the toilet." Lee didn't say another word. He seemed satisfied to sit in the chair, drinking.

"April," Chris said, "have you talked to John this evening? I mean since you got here."

"Yeah, I talked with him for a little while before the party started."

"Did he say anything about me? He hasn't said more than three words in a row to me since he got home. Is he mad at me?"

"Why on earth would he be mad at you? I know he's mad, but he's mad at Rich, not at you. He probably just doesn't know what to say and is afraid he'll say the wrong thing."

"I wish I knew what to say," Chris said. "What words can I use to tell him how I feel? How could I convince him that I was being honest?"

"Chris, John will believe anything you tell him. He doesn't blame you for what happened. The things that Rich did couldn't possibly change the way he feels about you. You've known John for a long time now. Do you really think

37

that he would take sides against you? Besides, you don't need to be thinking about that right now anyway. You need to be thinking about yourself. Give yourself time to indulge yourself in all the pampering you're going to get over the next several weeks, maybe months."

"I don't have time for all that. I only have a week before I have to go back to work. I'm also going to have to find a place to stay."

"You don't need to do that. You can stay right here."

"I'd love to stay here, but I still don't think John's even going to want me around."

"Let's not go down that road again. You know, it's no wonder the two of you have never hooked up. You both go out of your way to find reasons to believe the other doesn't want anything to do with you, despite what everyone else keeps telling you. I think you're both cowards."

Lee at last had something to add to the conversation. "Why don't you just sit out the week here? I'd be willing to bet things will work out."

Chris wasn't so sure, but she didn't say so.

John didn't know if he should be frustrated or relieved. For more than an hour, he had been trying to get up to the house to talk to Chris, but he kept getting cornered by people who wanted to talk about what happened. He was frustrated that people wouldn't leave him alone long enough to see her, but he was also relieved because he had no idea what to say to Chris. He would have to talk to her soon though. Also, John didn't know if he should try to speak to her alone or if he should take someone like April with him. They needed privacy, but he wasn't sure if being alone with him would make her freak out or something.

John finally found an opportunity to slip away, only to see Lyssa heading towards the house. Although he wanted to be part of that conversation, it was one that really needed to be kept between those two. Instead, he turned and walked back to the table where a multitude of bottles were spread out to keep the party lubricated.

Shannon couldn't believe this was happening. After all his talk about not wanting to come to this party, Isaac was apparently having a better time than she was. He had wandered off to get some drinks over an hour ago and never came back. Twenty minutes later, she found him hanging all over some girl near the back of the barn. Shannon had suspected that he was cheating on her, but she never thought he would do that in front of her. So much for saving their relationship. To make things worse, she would still have to ride home with him in the morning because there wasn't anyone else who lived near her. It also left her alone in a crowd of strangers. The only other two people she knew here were John and Ricky. She didn't really dislike Ricky, but she didn't like the idea of hanging around while he was doing business, and John was nowhere to be found.

Shannon walked around inside the barn looking for John but couldn't find him. She then decided that she would check the house. She had just stepped outside the barn when John found her.

"Shannon, what are you doing here? I thought you left."

"No, I'm still here. I can't go anywhere until Isaac leaves."

"I saw Isaac about five minutes ago. He got into his car and left. I just sort of figured you went with him."

Shannon's face flushed with anger. "What do you mean 'he left'?"

"He just left." John was already more than a little drunk. "I saw him getting into his car, and I was going to remind him that everyone had to stay until morning, but he drove off before I could get out there."

"That's just great," Shannon yelled. "First, he doesn't even want to come, and then he dumps me for some tramp and leaves me stranded here. Now what am I supposed to do?"

"Take it easy, Shannon. We'll get you home one way or another. Why don't you come up to the house? There's plenty to drink and not nearly as many people. You can just take it easy for a while, and we'll get you hooked up with a ride home tomorrow."

Shannon didn't trust herself to say anything. She simply nodded and walked off toward the house. It was just another good day gone bad.

April couldn't keep herself from crying, and Lee needed another drink, so they excused themselves when Lyssa showed up. They were sitting in the kitchen, knocking back some dreadful concoction that someone had made in a large bowl. It tasted awful and smelled worse, but neither of those was slowing anybody up from drinking it. April had already had more to drink in the last two hours than she had in the previous two months. At least the tears were drying up, although throwing up might make her feel better. She was trying to decide whether or not to have another drink, when she saw John come in with a black girl she didn't know. He pointed her in the direction of the kitchen before he went back outside. April decided to have another drink and was dipping her cup in the bowl when the girl walked into the kitchen.

"How are you doing tonight?" April asked as she raised the cup to her lips.

"I've had better nights," Shannon said as she grabbed a bottle of whiskey off the counter.

"I saw you walking in with John," April told her. "Are you a friend of his?"

Shannon jumped up to sit on the counter. "I guess you could say we're friends. We work together at the shop, but we don't really talk much outside of work."

April nearly tripped over the table leg as she walked around the table to where Shannon was. "You must be Shannon. John said that you might be coming. I'm April. I live down the street from John's step-father. …

Don't take this the wrong way, but I hope you weren't planning to hook up with John tonight."

"I wasn't planning on hooking up with anyone tonight," Shannon replied. "But, why, exactly, would that be a problem?"

"It's just that he's got enough to deal with right now without having a girl chasing him. Don't you think? I mean, he finally works up the courage to ask out the girl he's had a crush on for years, and she ends up getting raped. I'd say that's more than enough for anyone."

"Chris was raped?" Shannon was stunned.

"Yeah, you didn't know that?"

"No," Shannon said. "I knew a lot of people were upset, especially John, but nobody would tell me what happened."

"How'd you know it was Chris then?"

Shannon shrugged. "You said that he's had a crush on her for years. Who else would it be? She's all he ever talks about."

April rubbed her temples as she swayed on her feet slightly. "I'm sorry. I'm gonna have to sit down. I've had quite a bit more to drink than I'm used to."

"Don't worry about it," Shannon said. "I think I'll join you there."

Instead of sitting, April leaned against the counter and put her head up close to Shannon. "If you are looking to hook up with someone though," she said in a conspiratorial whisper, "I'd bet Rick would be willing to let you take your best shot. That boy really needs a girl holding his leash."

"Ricky? Do you mean the pusher?"

"Ricky's not a pusher; his old man is. Ricky just helps him out because it's better than getting knocked around."

"It don't matter, 'cause I ain't looking to hook up with anyone. I actually had a date when I got here, though he found himself another date since then, and I ain't seen him since."

"It's just not our day, sweetheart," April said as she sank to the floor. "It's just not our day." With that, she passed out.

※

"Hey Chris!" Lyssa said as she walked into the room. "What on earth are you doing up here? The party's out there."

Chris turned away from the window to look at Lyssa, who had been her best friend for as long as she could remember. The airy smile and clueless eyes plainly said that Lyssa didn't have any idea about what had happened. "I'm just not in the mood to party."

"What have you been smoking, girl? It's the last day of school. No more fat, old men and blue-haired, old ladies trying to fill your head with useless information. No more lullaby lectures and worthless word searches. It's over. We're free. Let's party. Here, I got you something." Lyssa handed Chris a gold-plated necklace with a heart-shaped medallion. Both of their names were engraved on the front and "BEST FRIENDS" on the back.

Chris held the necklace in her hands and fought back tears. It was nothing more than a small trinket, something Lyssa had picked up on an impulse at the mall, but it was the best thing that had happened to her all day. It wasn't long before she could not hold back any longer, and she broke down into tears and collapsed on the bed.

Lyssa scrambled to the bed and put her arms around her friend. "Chris, what's wrong? Are you okay?"

Chris sat on the bed, sobbing for several minutes before she could answer. Lyssa just sat there quietly, rubbing her shoulders. "I'm sorry," Chris said as she sniffed back more tears. "It's been a lousy day. Just give me a minute to pull myself together, and I'll tell you about it."

Chris stood up and walked over to the window where she had been standing and grabbed a tissue from the box that was sitting on the sill. She dabbed the tears from her eyes and began to tell Lyssa what happened. "I was all set to have the best day of my life when I got up this morning," she said as she lit a cigarette. "I didn't figure that anything could go bad today. Anyway, I went to the school early, like I always do, to work out for a while before school started. I ended with a few laps and was on my way to the locker room for a shower when I ran into Rich and a couple of his friends."

"What was Rich doing over at your school?"

"He wanted me to skip school with him and get a head start on the party. I told him no, because I'd been looking forward to today for a long time. I guess that wasn't the answer he wanted." Chris paused, finding it very difficult to continue. "When I wouldn't go with them, I guess they decided to have their party right there in the gym. Before I knew what was happening, they had a hold of me, and … and … they raped me." Again the tears came, and this time Chris didn't even try to hold them back.

"They raped you?" Lyssa asked in a choked whisper. "Why would Rich do something like that?"

"Yes, Lyssa, they raped me. I don't know why, but they did. They didn't get very far before they got caught, but that doesn't change what happened."

For the first time in her life, Lyssa was speechless. She couldn't bring herself to accept that her step-brother would do anything like that, but it was obvious that he had. Without thought, she walked over to where Chris was standing and again wrapped her arms around her best friend. Chris returned the embrace, buried her face in the nape of Lyssa's neck, and just let the tears flow. Lyssa stood there quietly, looking out the window and trying to give comfort to Chris, knowing that it wasn't really much help.

"I'm sorry, Lyssa, I didn't mean to spoil your night, but I'd rather you heard it from me than from somebody down there," Chris said. She stepped back a little, but not enough to pull away from the comfort of Lyssa's arms.

"There's nothing for you to be sorry for," Lyssa said. She was overwhelmed by emotions as she stroked Chris's hair. "It's not as though you intended for any of this to happen."

Neither girl said much after that; they just stood there looking at each other, trying to draw whatever comfort they could from one another. There were no words, no thoughts; they were just there. Chris had desperately needed somebody to hold her all day, but all of her other friends were either afraid to touch her, or she was afraid to touch them. Lyssa only knew that her friend needed her, and she wanted nothing more than to be there for her. What happened next took both of them by surprise. It wasn't something that either of them had planned or really even wanted. Before they knew what was happening, their lips met in a kiss. They were locked together like that for several moments before they simultaneously realized what was happening and stepped back from each other.

"What are you doing?" Lyssa asked in a quiet voice. "Is this what this was all about? Did you just want to get me up here all alone so that you could make a move on me?"

"No, that's not it at all," Chris said, confused and terrified. "I don't know what happened, it just did."

"You're a liar!" Lyssa yelled. "You made up that lie about Rich just so you could take advantage of me. I thought you were my friend." Lyssa ran from the room, slamming the door behind her. She was even more confused and terrified than Chris. Lyssa wasn't quite as clueless as she let on. She knew how most people felt about her, but as long as she had one real friend, Chris, she was all right with that. Now what was she supposed to do?

Chris started to go after her, but she had no idea what to say if she caught up to her. Instead, when Lyssa slammed the door, Chris collapsed on the floor and cried for all she was worth.

Brad and Kate had been at the party for just over an hour and still had not seen any of Brad's friends except Ricky, who was busy running the sound system and selling joints. Kate had bent, even broken, a lot of her own rules this night, but she was not about to go so far as to hang out with a pusher. She had a cup of something that tasted a lot like watermelon, and she drank it way too fast. She had never taken a drink before and was completely unprepared for how she felt afterward. Her head felt fuzzy, and she could barely stand. Almost as if he knew exactly how she felt, Brad put his arm around her and helped her over to a bench near the wall. Kate nearly choked when he helped her sit down and then handed her another cup.

"No way," she said as she pushed the cup away from her. "I don't think I could handle another one of those."

Brad handed her the cup again. "It's just RC, I promise. The carbonation will help break up the effects of the alcohol."

Kate took the cup and, after sniffing at it, sipped gratefully at the cola. "How'd you know I was going to need this?"

"I'm sorry. I should have warned you. That shooter you had was almost pure alcohol, and it was a pretty good sized cup. Just take it easy and you'll be fine in a minute or two."

"Can we go outside?" Kate asked. "It's suddenly very loud and very hot in here. I think I need some fresh air."

"That's probably a good idea. Why don't we head up to the house; that's probably where John and the others are." Brad held her hand as she stood and helped her through the door.

Kate was unsteady on her feet and had to focus all of her attention on not falling flat on her face. Even that was not enough when, about halfway to the house, Lyssa St. Thomas pushed her way past them, knocking Kate back on her pride. Kate couldn't tell what Lyssa was saying as she went by, but it was clear from her tone of voice that she was upset about something. There was no mistaking what Brad was saying to Lyssa as she disappeared into the barn. He was yelling loud enough that they probably heard him in town.

Brad bent over to help Kate up off the ground. "Are you all right?"

"I'm fine," Kate answered. "Nothing's hurt but my ego. At least I don't think so. Right now, I'm having a hard time feeling anything."

"Come on," Brad told her, "let's get you up to the house and get you another soda, or better yet, coffee. That should help"

"Actually, if you don't mind, I think that we probably ought to leave. This isn't at all what I expected."

"That's fine. We can stop on the way home and get something to drink. That is, unless you really want to just go home."

"I'd rather spend some more time alone with you," Kate told him. "I really should take some time to sober up a little before I go home to my parents. Do you know of any place on the way where we could stop for coffee?"

Brad put his arm around her and helped her walk out to where he was parked. "There's a little coffee shop in town. It's not exactly uptown, but the coffee's good."

When they got out to where Brad's van was parked, they found John sitting on the ground behind it, with at least three empty bottles laying around him and another half-empty bottle in his hand. Brad helped Kate into the van, and then went over to where John was on the verge of passing out. "Man, he's really twisted. He must have drunk all this in just the past hour or so, because he was stone sober when we got here." He grabbed John's arm and pulled it around his neck. John was just conscious enough to help out a little. "Do you think you'll be all right out here by yourself for a few minutes? I'm going to take John up to the house."

Brad was just turning around to take John up the hill when they saw Lyssa again. This time they saw her as she jumped into her car and sped off into the night. "That girl's going to kill somebody," Kate said, "and it's likely to be herself."

Chapter 5

It was almost noon by the time John finally woke up, but judging from the silence, it appeared that he was still one of the first to make it back to the world of the living. It was not the first time that he had ever waked with a hangover, but he had never had one this bad before. John felt almost as though he were still drunk. "What I need," he said to himself, "is a big cup of coffee. Maybe a pot or two." John fought his way out of bed and stumbled over to the window to look out at the yard. The bright sunlight hurt his eyes, but at least it looked like most of the partiers were still here. Fortunately, somebody had shut and locked the gate, though Brad's van was parked out by the road.

John turned away from the window and started to make his way downstairs. It turned out to be harder than it should have been. His head felt like it was ready to explode, and he had trouble keeping his eyes focused. To make matters worse, there were people passed out in the hallways and on the stairs. When he finally reached the kitchen, he realized that he was not the first person up after all. Brad was sitting at the kitchen table drinking coffee and reading the paper. He was also wide awake and smiling, which brought a rush of resentment in John.

"You look better this morning," Brad said as he looked up from the paper. "Not a lot better, but better."

"Thanks a lot," John said. "I have to look better than I feel. You look like you're in pretty good shape this morning, all things considered."

"Actually, I only had one drink last night."

"One drink? What in the world happened last night?"

"I had to take Kate home early, so I didn't want to drink a whole lot before driving all the way back into the city. Then I ended sitting on her front porch talking until about three this morning. By the time I got back, everyone was pretty much done for, so I just crashed on the couch."

John poured himself a cup of coffee and sat across from Brad at the table. "Thanks for making the coffee. I'm thinking I'm gonna need a bunch of this today."

"That's not surprising. You know better than to drink like that."

"I have no idea what you're talking about. I don't even remember most of last night."

"That's not really much of a surprise either. You drank three and a half liters of vodka last night, all in just over an hour. You're lucky you didn't kill yourself"

"At this point, I'm not really sure I didn't."

"Chris spent all night sitting in that chair at the end of your bed watching to make sure you didn't stop breathing. She was about the only person here who wasn't totally ripped."

"Have you seen her this morning? Do you think she might still be asleep?"

"Are you deaf as well as stupid? I just told you she spent the whole night sitting in your room. I don't think she slept at all last night. She went outside about twenty minutes ago. Don't ask, 'cause I have no idea where she went."

"That's okay. I don't think I could find her this morning if she was standing in front of me. Do you have any idea how many people are still here?"

"I'm thinking pretty much everyone's still here. Before Ricky locked the gate, maybe a half dozen or so slipped out, including Lyssa."

"How long was she here? Was she drunk when she left?"

"She wasn't here all that long, and I don't think she was drunk when she left. She did have a bottle with her, and I'm pretty sure she bought a couple of joints off Ricky."

"If she wasn't Chris's best friend, I would have told her where to get off years ago. I hope she didn't do anything stupid, but that is what she does best."

"I don't know that they're best friends anymore."

"What do you mean?"

"Apparently they had some kind of fight last night. It would seem that she threw a rock through Chris's windshield before she left."

"Somebody needs to slap that girl. I think I'll volunteer."

"You're going to have to take a number, 'cause I'm pretty sure there's a waiting list. I've wanted to slap her for years."

After that, other people began to come to and make their way to the kitchen for coffee or whatever else they could find. At first there was just one or two at a time, and then more and more as the afternoon wore on. John spent most of the afternoon sitting at the table making small talk with whoever was awake enough to string an entire sentence together. Some had obviously had a better time than others. There was one guy who didn't even know where he was or how he got there, and one girl—who had spent most of the night passed out in the middle of the barn—that went into hysterics when she woke up wearing nothing but her underwear. Overall though, it seemed as though nearly everyone had enjoyed themselves except the hosts.

John kept watching for Chris, but she didn't come back until everyone that was leaving was gone. John and the others were beginning to get worried, when she walked in a little after three. The only people left were Shannon and those who would be spending the week.

Chris was dead tired. She hadn't been able to sleep, so she sat up all night with John, making sure that he didn't die or anything. Although she had been up all night before, this was the first time she had done so when she wasn't high. She had a few drinks early on last night, but it didn't take long to figure out that it wasn't helping. So, she stopped drinking early so by the time Brad had dragged John up to his room, she was sober enough to keep an eye on him. Chris had spent the entire night sitting there watching John and trying to figure out where she was supposed to go from here. Even if she hadn't come up with any answers, thinking things through had certainly helped clear up her thoughts. When John started to stir in his sleep, she had left his room and headed downstairs.

When she got to the kitchen, she grunted at Brad and poured herself some coffee. Chris wasn't really in the mood to exchange small talk with anyone, so she stepped outside to get some fresh air. She had just about decided to go back inside and maybe get some sleep when she noticed that there were other people moving around, and she chickened out. Instead of returning to the house, Chris slipped through the gate and took a walk down the road to where it ended.

This was just about the perfect country road. It was paved with gravel, and the only person who lived on it was John, though it continued on about another mile or so past his house. Near the end of the road was a small bridge that crossed a deep gully through which ran a small, spring-fed stream. Just on the other side of the stream was a ten-foot electric fence with a large, chained gate. A sign on the gate said, "PROPERTY OF THE US GOVERNMENT; NO TRESPASSING!" Chris had no idea what was on the other side of the fence, but on this side, it was just her and the sound of water rushing over rocks below.

Chris sat on the bridge with her feet hanging over the side for the next few hours, just watching the water tumble over the rocks. It was starting to get dark when she decided to head back to the house. This time of year, sunset was not for several more hours yet, but out here in the sticks, the sun could only penetrate the trees when it was almost directly overhead. When she got back to the house, the last car was just pulling out of the driveway. Although she was still terrified of being around other people, even her best friends, she swallowed her fear and walked into the kitchen where the others were sitting.

"It's about time you decided to come back," April said as she walked in. "We were getting worried about you."

"I wasn't up to dealing with all those people, so I decided to go for a walk."

"Where'd you go?" Ricky asked. "There aren't that many places to walk to around here."

"I just went down to the end of the road and sat on the bridge. I hope you guys don't mind, but I need to go to bed; I've been up for almost two full days now."

"You go on and get some sleep. We were just talking about going to get something to eat. We could bring something back for you if you want," Ricky said.

"Are you going to the Route 104 Diner?"

"There's nowhere else to go, unless we want to drive all the way into the city," John said, "and my stomach won't wait that long. It's beginning to think my throat's been cut."

"I don't think I'm up to the 104. You guys go ahead; I ate a few hours ago. If I start getting hungry, I'll just make myself a sandwich or something." With that, Chris grabbed a warm can of Dr. Pepper off the counter and headed up to her room.

"If we're going, let's go," Brad said. "You can all ride in my van; there's plenty of room."

"Sounds good to me," John said. "I'm still not up to driving anywhere."

"You know, I think I'm gonna stay here with Chris," April said. "I'm really not all that hungry, and I don't feel right leaving Chris here by herself."

"You're probably right, but are you sure you want to stay here? If you want to go, I could stay," Ricky said. "Going out was your idea in the first place."

"I'm sure. Nothing personal, Ricky, but I don't think that a guy is who Chris needs to be alone with. Just bring me back a hamburger or something. You might want to go ahead and bring something back for Chris also, because I don't really think she ate something."

"All right then, we'll see you in about an hour or so. Hopefully it won't be much longer than that," Brad said. "Come on guys, let's get going."

It was very seldom that Kate slept past seven. This morning it was almost eight when she got herself out of bed. Last night had to have been the longest night since the creation of the world. She still did not know what to think about everything that happened yesterday. On the one hand, yesterday had been a complete tragedy. One of Brad's friends had been raped, another of

Brad's friends just might have killed himself with alcohol poisoning, and she wasn't sure if Brad had a good enough time to ask her out again. She also had no way of knowing without going back out to where the party was. Kate had also tried her first drink last night, an experience that would likely make her stomach woozy every time she thought about it for at least the next year or so.

On the other hand, despite all the chaos, Kate had a really great night. After months of trying, she finally got to go out with Brad. The date hadn't exactly been like something from a movie, but it had been great. They had stayed up until three this morning, just sitting out on the porch talking about anything and everything. She had been slightly nervous that he would make some kind of move on her, but he had kissed her and let it go at that. Of course, how far Kate should let it go was yet another problem; one of no small dimensions. That, however, was something that they would just have to work out as they went along. Honestly, she wasn't even sure if he would ask her out again. She'd been out with guys before, but she had never had a second date with any of them, so she didn't know how to gauge it. For her, the night had been wonderful, but she couldn't even begin to guess how Brad felt about it.

When she walked into the kitchen, her father had already left for work, and her mother was sitting at the table reading. "It's about time you decided to join me. For a while there, I thought you were going to sleep all day."

"Believe me, Mom, I thought about it."

"What time did Brad finally leave last night?"

"I finally made him leave around three. He still had to drive all the way back out into the country, past that little town out there by the river. I just hope that he made it back all right."

"Why'd he have to drive all the way out there? I thought you said that he lived just up the road."

"He does, but he's staying for a week with his friend who lives out there."

"Your father and I prayed all night for you last night. Dad wasn't real sure what to think about Brad when he came to pick you up. He sure was proud when he brought you home early, though. He talked about that for at least an hour before we went to bed."

Kate got out a bowl and a box of cereal and began to fix herself some breakfast. "Well, things didn't really turn out like we had planned on, but it still turned out okay. I never thought that we would have so much to talk about, but I never ran out of things to say, and he just amazed me with some of the things he knew. I think he's read just about every book that's ever been written."

"Well, I'm glad that the two of you had a good time. Did he ever tell you why he was late?"

"Yeah, it had to do with something that happened to one of his friends. It was pretty awful, and I really don't feel comfortable talking about it." Kate looked down at the paper sitting by her dad's seat and saw the headline about it. She slid the paper over to where her mother was sitting. "Here, you can read about it if you want to. I don't know how accurate it is. I didn't get the full story, just the basic stuff."

"I'll read about it later. You know that I don't like reading the paper until I finish my morning devotionals," she said, patting her Bible. "What are your plans for today?"

"I'm supposed to go over to the church later this morning and talk with Sister Shelly about that scholarship. I was thinking about going to see a movie after that. I'm not working tonight, so I don't know what I'll be doing later, at least until Brad calls."

"Just don't you go getting yourself dependent on him to call you every day. I'm not going to have you sitting around the house all day, waiting for some boy to call. No boy in the world is worth all that nonsense."

"I won't, Mom, I promise. I'm still going to hope he calls, though."

───※───

April had made just enough noise after everyone left to make sure that Chris would know that she was still here. She had seen Chris come to the top of the stairs, looking to see who was hanging around. After that she heard Chris turn on the water for a shower. April went into the living room and turned on the TV. The worst part of staying out here for the next week was that the cable company didn't come out this far. There was nothing on the local channels except for the news, but it was better than nothing. At least she thought so at first, but the top story on every channel was about "the brutal assault at one of the local high schools." She didn't think she could handle hearing that, and definitely didn't want Chris to hear about it, so she shut it off and went looking for something to read.

The one thing that you could always be sure to find when John was around was books. April picked up an old copy of Ibsen's *Ghost*, which was one that John always talked about, and sat down on the overstuffed couch and tried to read it. After a few pages, she realized that she and John had very different tastes in books. She almost cried for joy when she heard a car pull into the driveway. The others couldn't be back already, but it gave her something to do.

The girl who got out of the little Cavalier was someone she didn't know, but April thought she recognized her from the party. April figured that she had probably lost something, or she would not have come all the way back out here. April walked out onto the porch to meet her. "Can I help you find something?"

"I'm looking for Brad Randolph. Is he here?" the girl asked.

"No, he and some of the others ran into town to get something to eat."

"Do you think they'll be back soon?"

"It's hard to say for sure. It depends on who the waitress is. Is there something I can help you with?"

"Not really, I just wanted to talk to him. My name is Kate. Could you tell him I came by?"

"Are you the girl he was here with last night?"

"Well, we weren't here very long, but yeah."

"I thought you looked familiar, but we never got a chance to meet. If you've got the time, you can come in and wait for him. I'm not sure when he'll be back, but I could use some company."

"I've got time. What'd they do, run off and leave you here by yourself?"

"Not really. I guess you could say I'm babysitting. Chris didn't want to go, and I didn't think she should be sitting here by herself. The problem is that she's upstairs trying to get some sleep, which leaves me pretty much on my own. At least, I was until you showed up. Come on in."

Kate followed April through the front door and into the living room. "How is Chris?"

"Well, all things considered, I'd say she's doing all right." April pointed at one of the couches. "Go ahead and have a seat. I'm going to get an RC. Can I get you one?"

"No, thanks. I just finished a drink."

When April disappeared into the kitchen, Kate sat on one of the over-stuffed couches and took the time to look around. She didn't know what she expected, but it certainly wasn't what she was looking at now. The room was neat, though there were a couple of empty bottles that hadn't made it to the trash. The furniture seemed fairly new with the exception of a couple of antiques. The walls held up landscape paintings rather than posters of rock bands. It looked more like her mother's living room than that of a teenager.

April came back in and sat down on the other end of the couch and made herself comfortable where she could face Kate. "I don't think I introduced myself. My name is April. I live down the street from John's step-father. You must have really had a good time with Brad last night if you drove all the way out here just to see him."

"I did have a good time, but mostly I just wanted to make sure he got back all right last night. He didn't leave my house until late this morning, and I was sort of worried and had no idea how to get in touch with him."

"He's fine. In fact, I think he was the only one here this morning that didn't have a hangover. I think there's a lot more to you being here than just checking on Brad, though. I know that Brad really had a good time."

"Do you think so? I had a hard time telling if he was enjoying himself or not. I never really thought he would ask me out at all, so I figured that a second date might be too much to ask for."

"Girl, you're all he's talked about all day. I'm telling you, if he doesn't ask you out on a second date, I have no idea what's wrong with him. He's not nearly as tough as he'd like you to think he is, though."

"You know, I suspected that, but he really showed me that last night. We talked about everything, including a lot of things he never talked about at school. I never would have thought that he's been working to support his mother."

"Yeah, that's not really something that we talk about much, but his mother's pretty much been a basket case since his dad walked out a couple of years ago. She's on all kinds of medication and can't keep a job for very long, and if Brad doesn't buy the groceries, then his little sisters end up going hungry. That's why he's missed a lot of school. He's been working at a packing plant in the bottoms at night. I imagine he's had a hard time staying awake during school."

"You know, I've been putting myself in his way, trying to get him to ask me out since the day I met him, but until last night, I wasn't really convinced it was a good idea, if you know what I mean. It wasn't so much that he was different as it was that there was a lot more to him than he ever let on before."

"Don't worry about Brad, Kate. All you have to do is make sure he knows you're still interested, and I'm sure he'll respond. Enough about him though; we both know *him*. I've never heard about you before last night. If Brad's finally got himself a girlfriend, I need to hear all about it. So, talk to me. I need to hear your whole life story."

"Come on, you don't really want to talk about me, do you?"

"You better believe I do. I've made it my life's work to make sure everybody's all matched up. I haven't had time to fix Brad yet—I've been overloaded dealing with John and Chris—but I still need to know what's going on."

"There really isn't all that much to talk about. I've lived in the same place my entire life. I used to go to New Life Academy until my parents couldn't afford the tuition this year. About the only other thing there is to know about me is that if Brad really wants to go out with me again. It'll be a first for me—I've never had a boyfriend before."

"Get out of here! You're not serious, are you?"

"Yes I'm serious. I've gone out with a few guys, but never more than once. They just don't seem all that interested in a second date."

"You've got to be kidding me. Girl, you've got it together. I can't believe that guys aren't chasing you all over town."

"At first, everything is okay, but they all seem to lose interest when they find out that I take my Christian faith seriously."

"Are you really a Christian?"

"Yeah, is there a problem with that?"

"No, it's just that I don't know too many teenagers who could honestly say that. It's sort of hard for me to picture Brad going out with a Christian."

"I know what you mean there. That's why I never really expected him to ask me out in the first place. You wouldn't think that the two of us have anything in common. If you really think about it though, there's a lot more to all of us than the labels we're given. Brad and I got along fine last night, and we had all kinds of things to talk about. I'd sort of like to think that we could find a whole lot more to talk about."

"I think it's great. I didn't mean to sound like some sort of freak or anything; you just sort of caught me off guard. I mean I go to church with my parents, but I couldn't say that I'm a Christian. Actually, though, I think it might be good for Brad."

"What about you, do you have a boyfriend?"

"Sort of. I've been dating Lee for about a year now, but it's more like we're just really good friends. I mean, we don't even hold hands anymore. I've thought about breaking up with him, but I do like him."

"Do you think he'd be real upset if you did break up with him?"

"Not really. It'd probably bother me a lot more than it'd bother him. I just don't have the guts to do it and end up alone."

Kate laughed in spite of herself. "You're quite a match-maker aren't you?"

April laughed as well. "You're probably right. Maybe I should just give up on the whole thing, but I'm having too much fun with it."

The Route 104 Diner could never be accused of impersonating a four-star restaurant, but the food was decent and there was plenty of it. It was also within everyone's price range. The fact was that the place was a dump. The tables were clean, but they were old and dingy. Many of the mismatched wooden chairs were split down the seat, which often left the unwary with a splinter. Only the big plate-glass window in front was new; everything else was showing its age. Despite the aging, the 104 was comfortable. It didn't have the sterile, uniform appearance of someplace like McDonald's or the expensive, intimidating look of the restaurants downtown. It was almost as if you had been invited into someone's home. The walls were paneled in walnut, the tables were made from cedar, and most of the chairs were chestnut. It was the sort of place where you could sit down and enjoy a meal with good friends—as long as you were careful about the splinters.

"So, what are we doing this week?" Brad asked.

"There are still a few things I want to do with the house, but mostly we're just going to be hanging out," John said.

"I might be able to get us tickets for the Rush concert Saturday," Ricky told them. "I don't know of anything else going on, though."

"There's some sort of street fair going on in Clayton all week. I don't know if anything there is worthwhile, but it might be interesting," John said.

"What about tonight?" Lee asked.

"We could always go swimming," Brad said. "It's warm enough that we could splash around in the swimming hole for an hour or so."

"I can't," Ricky told him. "I have to take all the equipment back to my dad tonight. He's got something scheduled in the morning, and I want to unload all that cash."

"And I still have to get Shannon here home," John said. "If the rest of you want to, feel free."

"Why doesn't she just stay for the week like the rest of us? I'm sure the girls would enjoy the company," Ricky added.

"That sounds good to me," John replied. "What do you think, Shannon?"

"I'd have to check with my folks, but it sounds like fun. I still need to go home for a while, though. I don't have anything but the clothes I'm wearing. I'm thinking they might get a little rank after another day or two. They're already getting pretty rank."

Ricky took another drink to wash down the last of his fries. "Instead of a bunch of us driving in all different directions, why don't you just let me take Shannon home? She could ride with me to drop off the van and pick up my car, and then we can head over to her house so she can pick up whatever she needs for the week. We could probably be back by a little after ten. That is, if Shannon doesn't mind ridin' with the lunatic fringe."

"I guess that's all right, just as long as I don't have to spend too much time in that van, and you don't plan on doing any business in it between here and there."

"Nope, I ain't doing any more business for Pops. If anyone's interested, they know where to find him. With any kind of luck, I won't even remember anything about that van this time tomorrow."

"Do you need any help loading the van?" Lee asked.

"Nope, it's already loaded. All we have to do is get on the road. That is as long as John-Boy here hasn't lost my keys again."

"I know exactly where your keys are. They're on my dresser. And would you please stop calling me John-Boy? That really irritates me."

"I know that. Why do you think I do it? You have to admit though, that place of yours does look like the house from *The Waltons*." There was a general agreement and a lot of laughter on that one.

"If everyone is done," Brad said, "I'll go check on those burgers for the girls, and then we can get out of here."

"I'm done," Shannon said as she pushed her plate toward the center of the table. "That was pretty good, though I wouldn't have believed it when I first set eyes on this place. I was sort of wondering where you guys were taking me."

April and Kate quickly became good friends. As they waited for Brad and the others to get back, they talked a lot about Brad and the other boys they knew. When the group walked through the door, April and Kate were laughing so hard that they were literally in pain. "It's about time you got back," April said as she wiped a tear from her eye. "We were just about to send out a search party for you."

"Hey, Kate," Brad said, "I wasn't expecting to see you here."

"I just wanted to talk to you, make sure you made it back okay. But I didn't have the number out here, so I just decided to come on out. I only got lost once."

"How long have you been here?"

"I got here maybe an hour ago. I've been talking with April."

"We talked all about you, honey," April said. "We've got big plans for you."

"Oh, that's great. Maybe I ought to run away."

"Don't do that," John said. "If she's working on you, maybe she'll leave me alone."

"Don't hold your breath on that one, John," said Lee. "You're her favorite project. She'll always have time for you."

"Do you guys want me to leave," April asked, "so you can talk about me some more?"

"That's all right," Ricky told her, "I think we're done now."

"Not to change the subject or anything, but is Chris still asleep?" John asked.

"I think so," April replied. "I know she's upstairs and that I haven't heard anything from up there since before Kate got here. Did you bring me back some food? I'm about ready to starve here."

Lee handed her a Styrofoam box. "Here you go—Route 104's finest burger. It stopped mooing about five minutes ago."

"Um, um, just the way I like it," April said, taking the box from his hand.

"I need my keys, John. Shannon and I need to get on the road."

"I'll be right back," John said before bounding up the stairs.

"You know, I never did get an answer to my question about going swimming. Any takers?"

"Yeah right, Brad," April told him. "None of us have a bathing suit. What do you expect us to wear, our birthday suits?"

"A guy can dream, can't he? I'm serious, just put on a pair of shorts and a T-shirt, you'll be fine. We can build a bon-fire and get John to play his guitar. We'll just hang out and have a good time."

"Actually, that doesn't sound like a bad idea," Kate said. "At least the bon-fire part."

"There, see, we can go down and build a bon-fire, and anyone who wants to go swimming with me can. How's that sound?"

Lee threw in his opinion, "Sounds like a plan to me."

April finally gave in. "Fine, I'll go, but there's no way I'm going swimming with you bunch of animals around."

Just then, John called down from the top of the stairs. "Hey Ricky, come catch your keys."

Ricky caught his keys when John tossed them down. "Come on, Shannon, let's get rolling. I want to get this over with."

"I'm ready," Shannon replied as she followed Ricky out the door.

After they left, April poked Kate in the ribs. "See, I told you those two would get along. I'd say I hit that one right on the head."

Chapter 6

As John was heading back downstairs with Ricky's keys, he was stopped in the hall by Chris, who was standing in the doorway to her room. "I need to talk to you for a few minutes, John. Can you come in here for a while?"

"Sure, just let me throw Ricky's keys down to him, and I'll be right with you." John went to the top of the stairs and yelled down at Ricky to come catch his keys. After he had thrown them down, John returned to Chris's room. She had left the door open, but had gone back inside and sat down in an old armchair in the corner. John entered the room and leaned back against the wall next to the door. "So, what did you want to talk about?"

"Why don't you close the door and come over here where I can talk to you. This is just between you and me, and I really don't want anyone to overhear our conversation as they're walking past the door."

"Are you sure you're comfortable with that?" John asked. "I don't want to upset you or anything."

"I'll be fine, just do it," Chris answered. "I think I'm past the hysterics part of this. Right now, I just need to talk."

John closed the door and walked over and sat on the floor near where Chris was sitting. "Is there something wrong? I didn't do anything out of line did I?"

Chris put her feet up on her chair and wrapped her arms around her knees. "First of all, I want to thank you for everything you've done for me the past couple of days, and no, you haven't done anything wrong. You've gone out of your way to help me through a very rough time, and I really appreciate it. I also want you to know that you guys don't need to be so paranoid around me.

GEORGE FITHEN

I know very well that you, Ricky, April, and the rest of the crew down there had nothing to do with what happened. You guys are my best friends, and I've trusted you with a lot. None of that changed yesterday morning."

"I'm sure all that's true, Chris, but it's obvious that you're still hurting, and none of us want to do anything to make it worse. Even now, you're sitting there all balled up like you're afraid of me, and you keep looking at the window like you want to jump through it. None of us have any experience with this kind of thing, and it's going to take us some time to work our way through all the chaos. I can only imagine what it's taking for you to be this brave, but I don't know if this tough front you're putting up is going to help."

"I know all that, and that's part of what I wanted to talk to you about. When all the dust clears, what happened yesterday really isn't anything new. It's just more of the same thing I've been getting at home for years now. What I need more than anything else right now is to have my friends here for me, and for them to not be afraid I'm gonna break if they look at me wrong. Maybe I am still a little freaked out, but you don't look at all like you're comfortable here, and this is your house. I don't want you to be afraid to talk to me, or to be around me, or to touch me."

"You know we're always here for you, but I guess we could do a better job of showing you that. Is that what you wanted to talk to me alone about?"

"No, that was just the warning shot. What I really wanted to talk about was something that happened last night."

"Do you mean the fight you had with Lyssa?"

"That's part of it, but it wasn't really a fight. What I need you to do is to just listen until I finish my story. I just need to talk about it, and you're the only one I can think of who's not going to get all freaky on me. It's going to be hard for me to get through this, so please, just listen for a while. Can you do that for me?"

"Whatever you want."

"Last night, when Lyssa came up here, she had absolutely no idea about what happened. You know how she is; she probably heard people talking but just tuned it all out because they weren't talking about her. I know that a lot of people don't like her and that she's self-centered, but she was the only friend I had for a long time after my father died. I'm probably the only real friend she's ever had. She's always been there for me when I needed her, and I owe her a lot."

Chris took a deep breath and barreled on. "Anyway, I was sort of glad that she hadn't found out yet, because I didn't want her to hear it from someone who would hold it against her just because Rich is her step-brother. It was bad enough for her to accept coming from me. It was the first time I can remember that she couldn't think of anything to say. The only thing she did was to come over and give me a hug. It was the first time all day that anyone touched me just because. At the hospital I was just a patient. For the police and paramedics, I was just another victim. For Rich, well I don't really know what I was for Rich, but those were the only people who touched me all day until Lyssa showed up.

"When Lyssa hugged me, any control I had over my emotions just sort of fell apart, and all I could do for the longest time was hold on to her and cry. I don't know how to explain what happened after that, but it just felt so good to have someone who cared about me, who just wanted to lend some comfort like that. Everyone else seemed afraid they were going to make me freak or something, especially the guys, and they didn't come within four feet of me. I don't know if Lyssa just wasn't thinking about what she was doing or what, but that hug was the one thing I needed more than anything else. I was terrified that she was going to let go. For the first time all day I felt safe and loved. Before I even knew what was going on, I was kissing her."

Chris held her breath and looked at John but couldn't tell what he was thinking. "When I realized what I was doing I stopped, and so did Lyssa. I can't really blame her for the way she reacted; I guess it was just too much for her to deal with at one time. Anyway, she did the one thing I was most afraid of—she let go. For a while, she just sort of looked at me. I could tell that she was scared and confused. I was too. That's when she started yelling and calling me names, but that didn't hurt nearly as much as her letting go. She stormed out of here, and I don't know where she went or what she did after that. I wanted to run after her, to tell her I was sorry and make things right between us again, but I couldn't. I just collapsed on the floor and cried, and that's where I stayed until I heard Brad hauling you up the stairs.

"It was just something that happened, and I don't know why. I'm not gay; it's just what it is. That was when I began to understand what kind of effect this was having on other people. First, Lyssa freaks on me, and then Brad drags you up here—and you were barely breathing. In all the time I've known you, you've never even come close to doing anything like that before. Even Brad, the "Ice Man," was afraid to say anything to me. I could see it in his eyes.

"I've never said this about anyone before, but I hate Rich. Not because of what he did to me, but because of what he did to the people who mean the most to me. I also have to apologize, because I was thinking some pretty awful stuff about you yesterday. I thought that the reason you were avoiding me was because you were blaming me the way my mom does. I didn't think you wanted anything to do with me anymore. ...

That's pretty much how my day went. How bad did I mess things up?"

John took a few moments to collect his thoughts before he answered her. "In the first place, Chris, you didn't mess anything up. I doubt that Lyssa freaked out the way she did because of anything you did. Lyssa freaked because she doesn't deal well with reality. Every time reality enters her precious little world, she lashes out at the nearest target. You know that as well as I do. You've just never been her target before. What I did last night was stupid, but it was me who did it, and it had nothing to do with anything that you did. It was all about what Rich did, and it was stupid because I was letting Rich make my choices for me. Everyone here has been affected by this, even Shannon and Kate, who I don't think you've even met. But it's not because you messed anything up. In a way, you were right when you said that it was Rich who did these things to us, but mostly we're doing it to ourselves by letting his actions make our decisions.

"The only way any of us are going to get through this is to stop worrying about Rich and what he did and why he did it. We need to make our own choices based on what we want. And, we need to do it together like the friends we are. You know, it never occurred to me that what you needed might be someone to hold you and make you feel safe. I don't think any of us did. You don't need to apologize for what you were thinking or feeling. At least you knew what you were thinking, which is something I can't say for myself. Right now I don't know what I'm doing, but I am trying. I'll do whatever I can to help you, but I'm just not sure what that is."

Chris unfolded herself from the chair and stood. "You can start by getting up here and giving me a hug."

John did not hesitate to do that. He quickly got up and wrapped his arms around her. Although he knew that it was entirely inappropriate, John could not help but enjoy the feeling of having Chris in his arms. There was a big difference between holding her like this, to comfort her, and the way he wanted to hold her. Comfort, however, would have to do.

"Thank you, John," Chris said quietly as she locked her arms tightly around his chest.

The moment was ended by a knock on the door. "Hey, Chris, is John in there with you?" April yelled through the door.

John reluctantly released Chris, walked over to the door, and opened it. "Yeah, I'm here. What's up?"

"We're going down to the swimming hole to build a bon-fire. You guys want to come?"

"That sounds good to me. How about you, Chris? Do you want to go or would you prefer to stay here and try to get some more sleep?"

"I don't think I could handle being isolated up here anymore. Besides, it might do me some good to get out and do something with my friends."

⌘

"I really appreciate you doing this for me, Ricky," Shannon said from the passenger seat of the van.

"It's no problem," Ricky said. "I just need you to do me a small favor."

"Sure, as long as I can."

"It's no big deal, actually. When we get to the house to drop off the van, I need you to go ahead and get into my car and wait until I drop off the keys and money to my old man."

"I guess. Any particular reason?"

"Well, my dad's got a problem with black people, and I can't say how he'll react if he sees you with me."

"In other words, he's a bigot."

"That's being a little too generous. He's just about the world's biggest jerk, all the way around. It's bad enough when he's sober, but by this time of night, he'll either be stoned or drunk. It usually makes him easier to deal with, unless something sets him off."

"I take it you and your dad don't get along very well."

"My dad and I don't get along at all, unless I've got cash for him. That's why I'm done with him after this. I have no intention of letting him sell me up the river like he did my brother, Chuck."

"What about your mom?"

"My mother hasn't said a word to me in three years, and that was just to tell me to get her a needle. My mom's been strung out for as long as I can remember. She's got more heroine in her veins than blood."

"So, you don't care if you ever see them again?"

"Why should I?"

"They *are* your family."

"No, they're my parents. My family is back there at the farm. John, Chris, Brad, April, and Lee—they're my family. Look, I don't know what things are like at your house, but at mine, the only thing the three of us have in common is drugs, and I don't use them."

"You don't get high at all?"

"Not for a long time now. I have no intention of turning out like my old man. I don't drink a whole lot either. I know that the others do, and that's fine, but it's not what I want out of life. We're here," Ricky said as he pulled into the driveway of a shabby looking ranch style house. "The Mustang out there in front is mine. Go ahead and get in; it's not locked. I'll be out in a few minutes."

"All right, but hurry and be careful."

"I'll be fine, go ahead."

Shannon got out of the van and walked over to Ricky's car and got in on the passenger side. Part of her felt ashamed for hurrying along and sneaking around as though she had to hide who she was. She had met bigots before, and her grandmother had taught her to look them in the eyes and show the world that she was every inch as good as they were. It helped somewhat that she was doing it to keep Ricky from getting beat. Shannon was sure that she would feel worse if someone got hurt for helping her out. She lit a cigarette and tried not to think about it as she waited for Ricky.

It did not take long for Lee to get a good fire going. He had built it in the center of a cleared area on the stream bank where it had carved a deep hole in the bed. "All those years of Boy Scouts do come in handy once in a while," he said as the flames reached up to waist level. They had brought a cooler that was filled with what was left of the beer and sodas from the party. Lee grabbed himself a beer before sitting down next to the cooler.

"I don't know about the rest of you, but I'm going swimming," Brad told them as he took his shirt off. "I've wanted to do this since the first time John brought us down here."

"I'd leave the shoes on if I were you," John told him as Brad started taking them off. "There's no telling what's at the bottom of that stream."

"I think I'm just going to sit here by the fire and have a drink," April said. "If I'm going swimming, it's going to be in a chlorinated pool with no fish."

"Cowards," Brad said before turning and running down into the water.

He got into the water up to about his knees when he tripped on something and went splashing, face first, into the stream. He came up quickly and hurried back to the bank. Once out of the water, Brad stood as close as he could to the fire. "Dude, that water is cold."

"What'd you expect?" John said, laughing. "It comes straight out of a spring about a mile or so up. It's like that all year long."

"How could you stand to swim in water that cold?" Brad asked, his lips shivering.

"It's a lot better in the middle of July. Have a beer and relax; we have all summer to go swimming. It was a good idea to come out here, though. I think this is my favorite place in the world."

"It's nice out here, but I'm still not going swimming in that stream until you can guarantee that there's no fish in it," April told them. "I have to admit, though, that Brad looked pretty cute as he was coming up out of the water. What do you think, Kate?"

"I think that I wouldn't mind seeing that again. I didn't know you could move that fast, Brad."

"Oh, you two are hilarious." Brad's voice dripped with sarcasm. "Maybe you ought to take that act out on the road."

"Well, Brad, I'll let the girls decide how cute you are," John said, "but that was the fastest I've ever seen you move."

"You're supposed to be on my side here, John. What do you say we turn on the radio and gets some tunes going? It's nice enough out here, but it's too quiet."

"You're not going to get any reception down here," John told him. "There's a cliff on three sides and absolutely nothing on the other."

"What about the tape player?"

"Did you bring any tapes, because I didn't," Chris said. "Just chill out. I think you can make it for one night without your tunes. This was your idea."

"What did we bring the radio for then?"

"We didn't, you did," Kate said.

"I think Brad's having a bad night," Chris observed. "First his girlfriend gets together with April for a conspiracy, and then no one thinks to warn him how cold the water is, and then he finds out there's no music. We're all feeling bad for you, Brad."

"You're enjoying my suffering, aren't you, Chris?"

"You better believe it."

When Ricky got into the car, his bottom lip was puffy and bleeding slightly. "Let's get out of here before I do something stupid."

"What happened?" Shannon asked.

"Evidently, he was waiting for me, and he was watching out the window when you got out of the van. He only hit me once before he passed out though, so I guess it wasn't all that bad. Let's talk about something other than my old man."

"All right, what do you want to talk about?"

"Well, you could tell me how to get to your house for one thing—all I know is that it's on the west side."

"It's easy enough to find. I live on 71st Street, right next to Jennings Park. It's the only house on the block; everything else is apartment buildings."

"That must mean that you're the richest family in the neighborhood."

"I guess you could say that. My dad works three jobs. None of them really pay all that well, but together we do all right."

"Three jobs? What about your mother?"

"My mom works for my grandmother at the store she owns. She doesn't exactly get paid, but she gets free groceries. She also gets the store when Grandma dies. It's not much, but it's better than a lot of the neighbors have. At least my parents are still married, though I don't get to see much of my dad."

"Sounds pretty good to me. At least it sounds like everyone gets along."

"It is good. I have a good family, and we all love each other. Of course, Mom's not going to be too happy about me wanting to stay out in the boonies for a week with a bunch of guys."

"Is she going to let you?"

"Yeah, I think she will, but she still won't be too happy about it. She basically trusts me, and she thinks John is an angel. She's been wanting me to trade in Isaac for John since she met him."

"When did your mom meet John?"

"When I started working at the print shop, my grandma decided to have all of her flyers, posters, and whatever printed there. My mom goes in there just about every week."

"Sounds like just hiring the right people has helped their business. Are your folks going to be able to help put you through college?"

"No, I won't be going to college for a while. They still have my two baby brothers to take care of. I could've gotten a partial scholarship, but we still couldn't afford the rest of the tuition. Like I said, my dad works a lot, but he doesn't get paid very well 'cause he doesn't know how to read. He really wants me to go to college, though. The reason I've been working is to save the money for tuition."

Ricky and Shannon continued to talk as they drove through the city to Shannon's house. When they got there, Ricky parked in front and turned off the engine. "Do you want me to stay out here?"

"No, come on in. I don't know how long it's going to take, and it might help my mother make up her mind if she meets you. If you stay out here, she might think you're hiding something."

They got out of the car and walked up to the house. As they started to climb the stairs to the porch, the door opened and Shannon's mother came out.

"It's about time you got home. When you said that you'd be out all night, I expected you to at least get home before dinner. We were beginning to get worried about you," Mrs. Dent said.

"Sorry, Mom," Shannon said as she gave her mother a hug. "Isaac ran off and left me, and I had to wait for a ride with someone willing to drive all the way back into the city. Ricky, here, was good enough to give me a ride."

"Good riddance to Isaac. Thanks for giving her a ride home, young man. Are you in a hurry to run off somewhere?"

"Not really; I got time."

"Then why don't you come in for a bit. Mr. Dent has the night off, and we always like to meet Shannon's friends."

Mrs. Dent led them into the living room where Mr. Dent was sitting in a chair watching TV. It was a good-sized room with wood floors, immaculate drapes, and worn furniture. "Dad," Mrs. Dent said, "I want you to meet one of Shannon's friends, Ricky. He was kind enough to give her a ride home."

Mr. Dent stood up from his chair and reached out to shake Ricky's hand. He was sure that Mr. Dent was just about the biggest man he had ever met in his life. Ricky only had to look into his eyes once to know that, while he may not be able to read, Mr. Dent was anything but stupid. "It's good to meet you, sir."

"It's good to meet you too. I don't get the chance to meet many of Shannon's friends, especially ones that don't live around here. Come on in and have a seat. Do you like baseball?"

"Not really—I mean, I like to play, but I've never been able to get into watching it. I actually prefer football."

"Me too," Mr. Dent told him, "but baseball will have to do until preseason starts."

"I guess that's true," Ricky said. "Of course, I don't get a chance to watch much of either one."

"Are you a working man, Ricky?"

"I used to work for my father until just recently, but I'm not really cut out for that line of work, so I'm going to start college in the fall. You know, work out what I'm going to do with the rest of my life. I'm thinking about going into teaching."

"What sort of work does your father do?"

"He owns a portable sound system. The money's all right, but you almost always end up working with a bunch of drunks, and I don't get along very well with drunks."

"Mom, Dad," Shannon said, "John is having a bunch of friends spend the week with him out at his farm, and he's invited me. Would it be all right if I spent a few days out there? At least until I have to go back to work on Monday?"

"I don't know," Mrs. Dent said. "That sounds a lot like a recipe for trouble."

"What kind of trouble can we get into all the way out in the sticks?" Shannon asked. "I'd be sharing a room with another girl, April probably, and there's not going to be all that many of us out there—six or seven at the most."

"What are you going to do out there for a week?" Mr. Dent asked.

"We really haven't made any plans," Ricky answered. "We probably won't be doing much of anything really, except for staying up late and sleeping until noon. We'll probably spend some time working on the house. John just moved in there a couple of months ago, and it had been empty for years before that. There's still a lot that needs to be done."

"You're not going to be partying every night or anything are you?" Mr. Dent asked.

"No, we had our fill of that last night, and it'll be a while before anybody is feeling up to that again. Besides, one of the girls who'll be staying out there, Chris, has had a rough time recently, and I know she's not up to that."

"I don't know that I like the idea all that much," Mrs. Dent said. "A bunch of kids on their own like that. All kinds of things could happen."

"I'm not going to do anything stupid, Mom, I promise. Besides, I just broke up with Isaac, and it might do me some good to get away from him and his friends for a while."

"If there's any trouble," Ricky told them, "the sheriff lives just over the hill, and there's a gate between his place and John's. He can be there in about five minutes. In fact, he usually comes by at least once a day anyway. I don't think he's real sure if he trusts a bunch of teenagers out there either."

"What about the boys?" Mr. Dent asked. "I don't want any of them trying to take advantage of my Shannon. Do you have any interest in her, Ricky?"

"Oh, I don't know about that. I mean, I think she's very pretty, but we really don't know each other well, and she did just break up with her boyfriend. I might ask her out sometime, but I don't think it'll be this week."

"I'm not really convinced that it's a good idea," said Mrs. Dent, "but as long as you promise to stay out of trouble, and if it's all right with your father, I guess it's all right with me."

Mr. Dent stood by his chair for a while and looked first at Mrs. Dent, then at Ricky, and finally at Shannon. "Normally, I would say no, but nothing would make me happier than for you to get away from Isaac for a while—permanently if I could arrange it. You take care of my girl, Ricky. I'm going to hold you as accountable as I hold her."

"Thank you, Dad!" Shannon said as she ran over and gave him a hug. The hug lasted longer than Shannon had intended for it to, and Ricky was forced to look away when he saw tears in Mr. Dent's eyes.

"I guess you went and grew up on me when I was at work. I'm real proud of you, but I'm gonna miss my little girl."

"Dad," Shannon said as she broke away from her father, "I'm not going anywhere." She walked back over to where her mother was standing. "Thanks Mom. Everything's going to be fine, and I'll see you on Sunday. I have to go get my things together." Shannon turned and ran up the stairs.

"I'll go and give her a hand," Mrs. Dent said and followed Shannon up the stairs.

After the ladies had left the room, Mr. Dent sat back down in his chair and pointed Ricky toward the couch. "Have a seat, young man. You know, I'm not the smartest person you'll ever meet, but I know when someone's lying to me and when he's telling the truth. I also know that you weren't telling me the whole truth. I hope, for Shannon's sake, that what you're not telling me isn't something that's going to make me sorry I agreed to this. All I got is my family, and I don't want them hurt, especially my baby girl."

"There are things I didn't tell you, Mr. Dent, but I promise that they are not going to affect Shannon."

"Like I said before, I'm gonna hold you to that. Someday, you're likely to have a daughter of your own, and when you do, you'll understand how hard it is for me to let her grow up. I almost said no, but when I looked at her, my baby girl was gone and a young woman had taken her place. She looks just like her momma did. I could see in her eyes how much it meant to her to go, so I had to say yes. I believed you when you said that you weren't gonna ask her out, but I can see the look in your eyes that all young men get when they see a pretty girl. If you do ask her out, and I figure she'll say yes if you do, just don't hurt her."

Ricky was now officially uncomfortable. He had never even considered having this conversation. "To be honest with you, Mr. Dent, I really would like to ask Shannon out, but I don't think I could do that to her. I'm leaving for Colorado in a month or so, and I have no intention of ever coming back. I wouldn't feel right about getting involved with someone, knowing that I'm leaving."

"You have a few rough edges, kid, but I think you're gonna be all right.

Whether you ask Shannon out or not, I want you to know that you're welcome to come back here anytime."

"Thanks, I appreciate that."

They didn't say anything else to each other. Instead they sat there quietly watching the game and waiting for Shannon. When Shannon and her mother came back downstairs, they were each carrying a bag. "Could you take these out to the car for me, Ricky? I'll be out in a minute."

"Sure thing," Ricky said taking the bags. "It was good to meet you Mr. and Mrs. Dent."

Ricky walked out to the car and put the bags in the backseat. He then leaned against his white '71 Mustang and lit a cigarette as he watched Shannon talking to her parents at the door. Ricky considered Shannon to be one lucky girl. Her family didn't have a whole lot, but they didn't seem to need anything they didn't have, other than a few more hours in the week. Ricky just hoped that Shannon realized how well off she was.

After a couple of minutes, Shannon came down to the car, and her parents went back inside the house. Shannon didn't say anything at first; she just got in the car, as did Ricky. Only after Ricky had pulled away from the curb and was halfway down the street did she speak. "Thanks, Ricky. I don't know how exactly, but you seemed to come up with all the right things to say at the right times."

"I was just telling the truth. I didn't see any reason not to."

"When I saw that my father was home, I figured that there was no way I was going to be able to go. I think you're the first guy I've brought home that he didn't hate immediately, and we're not even going out."

"Your dad's a pretty smart guy, and all he wants is for you to be happy."

"I know, and he doesn't think that he's been able to do that for Mom. He thinks he's a failure. He's just never caught a break."

Chapter 7

Kate was up early, as usual, the next day. She had stayed out at the farm until nearly midnight and had left only reluctantly. She was now convinced more than ever she wanted to be Brad's girlfriend, but that wasn't the only reason she had not wanted to leave. For the first time since she had left the Christian school, she had found people who had accepted her for who and what she was and made her feel welcome. It didn't seem to bother them at all that Kate was a Christian, though it bothered her that they were not. It wasn't that she liked them any less; it was just that she wanted to share with them what she had. She also believed that the rough times they were dealing with wouldn't seem nearly as bad if they could just share their problems with God; and let him heal the wounds. She got herself dressed and wandered into the kitchen where her parents were eating their breakfast. "Good morning, Mom, Dad."

"Good morning, Kate. How are you feeling this morning?" her father asked.

"I feel all right, but I'm still a little groggy."

"You were out pretty late last night. What did you do all day yesterday?" her mother asked.

"I spent most of the day at the church, helping Sister Shelly in the office. Afterward, she took me out for dinner."

"What about last night?" Mr. Knight asked.

"Well, I decided to drive out and see Brad."

"I don't know that I like the idea of you driving all the way out there by yourself, especially to see a boy," Mrs. Knight told her.

"I understand that, Mom, but I really wanted to see him and let him know that I was interested in 'seeing' him again and find out if he was interested in 'seeing' me again."

"So, what did he say?"

"Nothing directly, but I got the feeling that he wants to see me again. Everyone else seemed to have that impression also."

"Who's everyone else?"

"They're Brad's friends. They're all staying out at John's farm for a week, helping him get it fixed up. Last night, we went down to the creek and built a bon-fire and talked and joked all night. They were all giving Brad a hard time about finally having a girlfriend. I had a really great time, and I made some really great friends. They asked if I could come back out this afternoon and help them."

"That's great, hon," Mr. Knight said. "What are they doing this afternoon that they need help with?"

"They're just doing work around the house, mostly painting I think. I take it that it was deserted for years before John moved in, and it still needs some work. I guess they've been working on it for months, mostly on the weekends, but there's still a lot that needs to be done. I need to ask your advice on something, though."

"Sure, sweetheart, what's the problem?"

"Did you read that article in the paper I pointed out to you, Mom?"

"Yes, I did. That poor girl has got to be devastated."

"They all are, Mom. They're probably the closest-knit group of friends I've ever met, and this is affecting them all. I really want to help them out, but I don't have a clue how."

Mr. Knight got up to pour himself another cup of coffee. "Are they Christians?"

"No, and that's the problem. I really want to witness to them and show where the healing is, but I just met them and I don't want to scare anyone off."

"From what I read," Mrs. Knight told her, "this is a group of kids that really need the Lord. Maybe that's where you're supposed to be. It's possible that God put you there at this time so that you could help them. Just talk to them. You don't need to share your testimony or anything, just be a friend for them and offer to pray for them. I think you'll be surprised at just how far an offer of prayer will go."

"I know you're right, but what happens if I offer and they start to turn cold on me?"

"When people are hurting," Mr. Knight told her, "they're usually grateful for your concern. They might not believe what you tell them, and they might not even listen, but they'll seldom turn cold on you. Your mom's right. I think God put you there for a reason. Maybe you're the angel he's sending to them."

"Just listen to your heart," Mrs. Knight added. "If you listen close enough, God will lead you through what to say and when to say it."

John felt much better this morning than when he did yesterday. Although he had slept later than usual, he was still up earlier than anyone else in the house. John liked being up early when it was quiet, and there were no distractions. It helped him clear his head and get ready for the day. Not that today was going to be anything special. They were just going to work on the house, but he appreciated the time anyway. He pulled on a pair of shorts, lit a cigarette, and walked over to the window to see how the day was going to be. Since he moved out here, he had remembered what his grandfather had taught him about reading the clouds, and what he saw this morning told him that it was going to rain soon, but not today.

John really enjoyed himself last night. By the time they had gotten back to the house, it was late, and everyone was tired. John was even pretty sure that even Chris had gone to bed and gotten some much-needed sleep. It seemed as though everyone had a good time, which was more than could be said about the party. There had been two extra people with them last night. He was really glad that Shannon was going to be staying for a few days. Her dry humor always made the days go better. He was not too sure what to think about Kate, though. She seemed nice enough, and she had really hit it off well with April, but there was something different about her. John liked Kate, and she was welcome anytime. He just didn't know what to make of her.

However much he had enjoyed himself or how nice the day would be, he still wasn't sure how to deal with Chris. She had made it clear that she wanted things to be like they had been, but John wasn't convinced that she was being honest with herself about that. When they were alone together, she had sat in a chair and wrapped her arms around her knees as though she were afraid of him. When they were down at the creek, she had kept a good distance between herself and the others. She also kept looking back over her shoulder. The problem was that he didn't know how he was supposed to treat Chris as he always had and still not upset her. Somehow, he would just have to work it out as he went along, because he was sure that there really wasn't an answer. John put his cigarette out in the ashtray on the sill and went downstairs to fix a pot of coffee.

Chris first woke up to the sounds of someone moving around in the kitchen right below her bedroom. She rolled over and sat on the edge of her bed and rubbed her eyes. Last night she had a really good time. It had helped a lot to be able to talk to John, and spending time with all of her friends down by the swimming hole had been great. She still wasn't feeling like herself, but she did feel a whole lot better. The thought of those hands all over her still made her feel dirty, and she still felt hunted, as though being tracked by some relentless sportsman. Chris was encouraged, though, that her friends still seemed to want her around.

Generally Chris liked mornings, but not this morning. The sun was too bright, and her thoughts were running away from her. Given her lack of sleep recently, it was still way too early for her. She was glad that she hadn't had anything to drink last night; it would just have made the sun seem brighter. After a few moments, she decided against getting up just yet and laid back down to get some more sleep.

"Morning, John," Shannon said as she walked into the kitchen. "How are you feeling today?"

"Good morning, Shannon, I'm fine. You look like you're feeling pretty good as well."

"I haven't felt this good in a long time. Is anybody else up?"

"No, the others probably won't wake up for a while. They're not exactly morning people. There's coffee ready if you want some."

"No thanks, I don't really care much for coffee. I prefer my caffeine cold."

"Well, there's RC and Dr. Pepper in the fridge if you want."

Shannon went over to the refrigerator, grabbed an RC, and sat down at the table across from John. "I've got a question for you. I know that Ricky's your best friend, but what's your honest opinion of him?"

"Why, do you like him?"

"I don't know. I didn't think I did, but after spending time alone with him last night, I don't know what to think."

"Ricky's sort of a lost soul. He's the best friend you could ever ask for, but there's something that he needs, and I don't think friendship is enough. You might have noticed that his family's sort of messed up. He's a good guy in a bad situation, and the sooner he gets out, the better off he's going to be."

"Isn't he out now, though? I mean, he's not going back there, is he?"

"Yeah, he's out of the house, which is good, but I don't know if that's far enough. Everyone around here knows him, and they know what he does, and as long as he's here, that's what they're going to associate him with. Did he tell you he was going to Colorado in the fall?"

"Yeah, he said he's going to start school there."

"He is. He got a scholarship to Colorado State, but he also got offered full scholarships to just about every college in this state. He knows he has to go, but he doesn't really want to leave. That's why he stopped getting high; he's trying to distance himself from his father. It's not really working, though, and he's going to have to leave the state. That's what I meant by getting out."

"Don't you think that he'd be better off staying here where his friends are? I mean, it sounds like he's running away, and that just doesn't seem like Ricky."

"Maybe he is running away, Shannon, but you have to pick your battles, and I don't think this is one that Ricky can win. Not right now anyway."

"It just doesn't seem fair that he's the one who has to go away. Especially since this is his home, and this is where his friends are. He told me last night that you guys are his real family. What's he going to have waiting for him in Colorado?"

"His future is in Colorado. A future without a past. I don't want him to leave either. I need him around to help keep me honest. Talking him into staying, though, would be selfish."

"If his friends are all he has, and if they're halfway across the country, what's gonna keep him honest?"

"I don't know, Shannon, I really don't. All I can tell you is that Ricky deserves a chance to be who he wants to be, not what other people think he is."

"What about Chris? Would you feel the same way if she told you that she needed to leave also?"

"That I don't know. If she thinks that's what she needs, then I'll do anything I can to help her."

"Even if it means you'd never see her again?"

"I don't have an answer to that, Shannon. I can't think of anything I want more than to be with Chris, except for her to be happy. If going away and never coming back is what makes her happy, then it wouldn't do me any good to make her stay, would it?"

"John, I think you're too smart for your own good. Maybe you should start thinking about things with your heart and turn off your brain for a while. What about your happiness? Doesn't that matter too?"

"No, it doesn't, not really. I mean, I couldn't be happy if my friends weren't. It's hard to explain, but like Ricky, all I have are my friends. I don't have any family, not even a worthless one like Ricky's. There are no brothers or sisters or distant cousins. All I have is a step-father who loved my mother, but resented getting stuck with me after she died. Don't get me wrong—Bill's a nice guy, but he didn't marry *me*. All that leaves is Chris, Ricky, Brad, April, and Lee. There is absolutely nothing I wouldn't do for them."

"I guess there's no way I could ever understand that. My mom's right about you, you know. You really are an angel."

Just then, Brad and Lee came into the room. "I'm telling you, dude, I ain't never heard nobody snore like you do," Lee was saying. "You woke me up four times last night."

"Nobody's perfect," Brad replied. "Morning, John, Shannon. Lee was just informing me how abused he is. Poor thing hardly slept at all last night."

"Is there anybody else up?" Lee asked.

"As far as I know, it's just the four of us. I figure Ricky and April should be up soon, but if she's smart, Chris will probably sleep for a while longer."

"I've been meaning to ask you about that," Brad said as he poured himself a cup of coffee. "I know that you had big plans to ask Chris out. Are you still thinking along those lines?"

"I don't know. When we talked yesterday, she told me that she didn't want us to treat her any differently than we had before, but the whole time I was in there, she acted as though she were afraid of me. I've been trying to work up the courage to ask her out for better than a year now. I don't think it would hurt to wait some more. What about Kate? Are you going to ask her out again?"

"I was planning on it. I wasn't real sure that she would want me to, but she gave me the impression last night she'd be okay with it. Kate's not the kind of girl you just ask out once. Relationships are important to her, and if it works out, I could live with that."

"Did you put something in this coffee, John?" Lee asked. "I think I'm hallucinating. I could have sworn I just heard Brad say he could date just one girl."

"I thought I heard the same thing. Maybe we're really still asleep and this is just a dream or something."

"Didn't you guys get enough of that last night?" Brad asked. "I like Kate. She's not like anyone I've ever gone out with before. Everything changes."

"Just giving you a hard time, dude. As far as I know, you've never gone out with the same girl twice before, so we have to take advantage of the opportunity when it comes 'round."

"Like I said, everything changes. Give it a rest, will you? At least wait until I've had a couple more cups of coffee. It's still too early for this."

"What about you, Shannon?" Lee asked. "Are you going to take a break from men for a while?"

"That depends on what comes up," Shannon answered. "I'm not going to turn a good thing down, but I'm not looking either."

Just then, April came in smiling. "Good morning, guys. How's everyone feeling this morning?"

"April," Lee said between sips of coffee, "I don't know how you manage to be in such a good mood in the mornings, but I wish you'd stop."

"You're just an ole grump in the morning, Lee. Is there any coffee left?"

"There should be enough for one more cup, but you get to make the next pot."

April poured herself a cup of coffee and began to make another pot. "So, what are we doing today, John?"

John drained his cup and sat back in his chair. "Painting. We should be able to get the rest of the house today. All that's left is that one area in the back. We shouldn't even need ladders. We'll just have to see how much time is left after that before we move on to anything else."

"When are we going to start on the basement?" Brad asked.

"Not today. I'm putting that off until last. I've been trying not to think about it."

"What's so bad about the basement?" Shannon asked.

"There's about a hundred and fifty years of accumulated family heirlooms down there," Brad told her. "A lot of it is probably worth some money, but a lot of it is also junk."

"Did you ever get that door in the back open?" April asked.

John got up and poured himself a cup of coffee from the half-brewed pot. "Yeah, I pried it open last week."

"Did you find anything good, or was it just more junk?"

"There's a bunch of stuff from when my grandpa was a kid in Germany. There was also some stuff from my great-grandfather too."

"What are you going to do with it? Are you going to get rid of it, or are you going to keep it?"

"I don't know, but I'm not going to worry about it now."

"Wouldn't most of that stuff just rot in the basement after all these years?" Shannon wanted to know.

"Normally, it would," John told her, "but this place has two basements. There's a regular basement, and then a sub-basement below that. The sub-basement is all damp and musty, but that helps make the basement a good storage place. Everything was sealed up pretty well also."

"What about bugs?"

"Oh, there are plenty of those down there," Lee told her. "There are enough spider webs down there to cover the house."

"That's why I've been trying not to think about it," John said.

Ricky then walked in and grabbed an RC from the fridge. His hair was a mess and he was in need of a shave. "Dude, I hate mornings. It looks like I'm the last one up again."

"Actually," Lee said, "I think you beat Chris this morning."

"Not really. I heard her moving around. She might have gone back to bed, though. I was seriously thinking about doing the same, but once I'm up, I usually can't go back to sleep."

It was late morning when Chris struggled out of bed and joined the others. Not long after that, they set to work, scraping and painting the house. It was hot, tedious work, but they had the radio on to keep them entertained and plenty of cold drinks to cool them off—sodas for Chris and Ricky, and beer for the rest. Around 1:00, Kate pulled into the yard and parked not far from where the work was going on.

"It's about time you decided to show up," Brad said as he walked over to where she was getting out of her car. "I was beginning to think you were going to skip out on us." Brad gave her a quick kiss and then took her hand and led her up to the house.

Kate said a quick, silent prayer for Brad's gestures and eagerly took his hand to follow him to where the others were hard at work. "I would have been here sooner, but I had to stop at the store to pick up a few things for my parents."

"Don't pay any attention to him," April told her. "We haven't even been at it for more than a couple of hours yet. We spent most of the morning goofing off."

"What do you need me to do?" Kate asked.

"I think we're pretty much set here, but Chris could probably use some help. She's in the barn mixing up paint," John told her.

"He's a slave driver," Brad said to her, "but we love him anyway. Go ahead. I better get back to painting or we'll be here all night."

In the barn, Kate found Chris sitting alone in the middle of the floor, stirring up the paint with an electric mixer. "I've never seen one of those used like that before."

"It sure beats doing it by hand," Chris replied. "John came up with the idea when we were working inside."

Kate knew she had to talk to these people, and Chris was probably the best person to start with. "Can I talk to you for a minute, Chris?"

"Sure, what's up?"

"I know that we don't really know each other very well, and you may not want to talk about what happened at all, but I want you to know that if you need to talk to someone, I'm here to listen."

Chris stopped the mixer and put it down near the can of paint she was working on. She didn't say anything at first; she just looked at Kate as if she were seeing her soul. "Thank you. It means a lot to have people to talk to, and actually, I do want to talk about it. That's the only way any of it makes any sense. I don't want to talk about it right now, though, because once I get started, I might not be able to stop, and there's a lot to get done today."

"I know. I just wanted to let you know that I'm here, and I also wanted to ask if I could pray for you."

"You want to pray for me? Don't waste your time. God gave up on me a long time ago."

"What in the world would give you an idea like that?"

"The good people down at Second Street Church. I went in there once and was told point-blank that there was no place for people like me in God's house."

"Well, they were wrong. God doesn't give up on us, Chris; we give up on him and each other."

Chris picked up a couple of the cans of paint. "If you really want to, go right ahead. I could use all the help I can get. Here, help me with these cans," she said, indicating the two cans she couldn't carry. The two of them each grabbed a couple of paint cans, and they walked off together toward the house.

Chapter 8

John was worn out. He had been working for a couple of hours and was hot and tired. He needed to take a break. He walked up onto the porch and sat in the cool shade. Then he grabbed a beer out of the cooler and used the sleeve of his T-shirt to wipe the sweat from his face. John was taking another long drink when Kate walked up onto the porch and joined him in the shade.

Kate's hair, which was always meticulously arranged, was damp and limp from sweat. She had been working as hard as everyone else, and she definitely looked like she was in need of a cool drink. Despite her disheveled appearance, however, John could see why Brad was so taken with her. Of course, there had to be more to it than just her looks. There was something about this girl that affected Brad in ways that John was at a loss to explain. John had never really paid that much attention to Kate, but he figured this was as good a time as any to get to know her a little better.

"How're you doing, Kate? You look like you're about ready to call it quits for the day."

"Just about. You know, I've never done this kind of work before. I never realized how hard it is."

"You should have been here a couple of weeks ago when we were tearing down some of the old outbuildings. It's supposed to be easier to tear something down than it is to build it, but someone forgot to tell those old buildings."

Kate laughed a little. "It sounds like you took on a little more than you realized."

John laughed as well. "If that's not the biggest understatement ever, it'll do until the real thing comes along. This whole place has been like that. It seems like every time we get started on a new project, we find that there are at least two or three other things we need to get done before we can finish."

"Are you starting to think you might have made a mistake taking all this on?"

"Yeah, sometimes I do, I guess. Mostly, though, I'm just impatient to get done with it all, at least the major stuff. My mom and I lived here long enough for me to know that with a house like this, the work is never really done. There's always something that needs to be fixed, adjusted, or redone. That's just the way it is."

"You lived here with your mom? I thought this was your grandparents' place."

"It was, but after my father died, my mom and I moved in with them here until she got remarried. Not long after that, they built the other house and left this one empty."

"Where's the new house?"

"It's on the other side of those hills over there, just off the highway. After my grandfather died, we had to sell it to pay everything off. That's where the sheriff lives now."

Kate was still standing just at the top of the stairs, leaning against the rail. "You really ought to get yourself something to drink," John told her, pointing at the cooler. "You're going to dehydrate if you don't."

"You got anything in that cooler besides beer?" Kate asked, walking over to it.

"There should be cans of RC and Dr. Pepper in there somewhere. If not, then I know there's some in the fridge. There might even be a Sprite or two left."

Kate found a Dr. Pepper near the bottom of the cooler and then closed it so she could sit on top of it. "I've been meaning to talk to you, John. Do you mind if I ask you a rather personal question?"

"No, I don't mind. What did you want to know?"

"Brad was telling me the other day that you've had a crush on Chris for a long time. I was just wondering how you felt about what happened the other day."

"Well, to be honest, I don't really know how I feel about it. At first, I was furious, and I think that if I had managed to put my hands on Rich at that time, I really might have killed him. Then, later that night, I really don't remember too much. I had way too much to drink because I thought way too much about it. Since then, I've been trying not to think too much about anything. Sometimes, I can't help but feel sorry for myself, but I try to put that away as much as possible because Chris is the one who really needs support just now, not me."

"Well, I won't argue with you about Chris needing her friends," Kate told him, "but if you really think about it, weren't you a victim of what happened as well as Chris?"

John took another drink from his beer and lit a cigarette as he thought about what Kate said. "You may be right about that, Kate, but if I stop to think about what I want or need, then I'd be taking away from what I can do for Chris. I'd give anything to make the whole thing disappear, to make it so that it never happened. I can't do that, though, so I'm going to do everything I can to help her put it behind her. There just isn't any time left over to worry about anything else."

"Have you thought of praying about it?" Kate asked.

"Praying isn't anything that I know anything about, Kate. Even if I did, I rather doubt that God would pay any attention to what I had to say anyway. In case you hadn't noticed, I'm not exactly what you would call a religious sort. God may listen to the prayers of people like Jimmy Swaggart, but I doubt he has time for guys like me."

"God has plenty of time to listen to your prayers, John, and he does listen, even if you're not Jimmy Swaggart. He just wants to hear from you. He loves you just as much as he loves anyone else. Religion doesn't have anything to do with it. What really matters is that you have the faith to believe in God and put your trust in him."

"Right there, you hit the core of the problem, Kate. I don't know that I have faith in anything anymore. I had little enough after my mother died, and after the other day, about the only thing that I have any faith in is that the world doesn't have any place for guys like me. I think it's great that you have all this faith, Kate, but I don't."

"Would it upset you to know that I was praying for you?"

"Actually, if that's who you are and what you believe, then I think it would bother me more if you didn't. If you really want to pray for somebody, though, you might get a better return if you put someone else on your list, like Chris or Ricky or someone."

"All of you are on my list; I don't have to limit it to just one name. You're a better person than you give yourself credit for, John. If you believe it or not, I think that God has taken a special interest in you. It just might be that you're the answer to prayer that God sent to Chris to help her when she needs it the most. Think about that. I'm going to go inside for a little while where it's cooler. Do me a favor and think about what I said. Don't just blow me off … or rather, don't just blow God off." Kate stood up and went inside, leaving John alone with his thoughts.

There was a part of him that wanted to laugh off Kate's ideas as foolishness, but there was another part that really wanted to believe that there was a God in the universe who cared about him and could help him sort things out. The one thing that really stuck out from the conversation though, was the idea that Chris wasn't the only victim. If that were true, and he had already begun to think that it was, then there were others in his little circle of friends who would need a lot of help coping. There were others who would need his help and support, and John did not know if he had the strength for that.

Shannon was inside sitting on the couch. She was used to hard work, but she was not used to working outside in the heat and had not thought to drink anything until she had gotten light-headed. She nearly passed out before Ricky practically carried her inside. He had been very insistent that she stay inside and drink something. At first, she had resented him treating her like a child, but now she was glad that he had. Shannon was feeling better, though still a little dizzy, especially when she tried to move too fast. She was just finishing up the last Sprite and had lit a cigarette when Kate came in and sat down beside her.

"How are you feeling, Shannon?" Kate asked as she set her drink down on the table next to the couch.

"I'm doing better, but I still feel like an idiot. I never even thought about getting myself something to drink. I guess I'll know better next time."

"You had us worried out there for a while. I was thinking that it's getting sort of late, and I'm getting hungry. I was wondering if you want to ride into town with me and see about picking up some pizzas or something."

"I think that's just about the best idea I've heard all day."

"Why don't you get ready, and I'll see about getting money from everybody. There's no way I could afford to get pizza for this group, and I don't think you could either. Just meet me out by my car." Kate left her soda sitting on the table and headed outside through the kitchen, which was the same way she came in.

Shannon put her shoes on and thought about going upstairs to get her brush but decided against it. She was a mess, but she didn't feel the trip upstairs was worth the effort right now. After they ate, she would see about taking a shower, but for now, anybody who saw her would just have to see her the way she was. She went out the front door and started walking out to where Kate's car was parked. Shannon hadn't gotten very far before Kate came around the corner to meet her. "That didn't take very long. Was everyone gathered on the porch or what?"

"No, John gave me fifty to pay for everything and told me where the best place was to get the pizza."

Shannon shook her head as she walked. "That boy's going to be broke inside a month the way he's spending that money."

"What do you mean?" Kate asked as they both got into the car.

"I mean, his grandfather left him a lot of money, but he didn't make him a millionaire. He's already spent most of that money on this house, but he's still spending it, mostly on everyone else. Did you know that he bought a car for Chris? I don't think he's given it to her yet, but he was talking about it the other day at work. I know that she needs it, but it wouldn't hurt for him to replace that old junker he's been driving around before he buys one for somebody else."

"Maybe there's more money than you think."

"That's possible I guess, but I rather doubt it. He's always like that. He buys lunch for everybody at work at least once a week. The money doesn't really seem to matter much to him, but once it's gone, he's not going to have anything to show for it."

Kate pulled out of the driveway and headed toward town. "How long have you known John and the others?"

"I met John a few months ago when I started working at the print shop, and Ricky just a little bit after that. The rest of them I met the other night at the party."

"That's strange. I would've thought that you'd been friends with them a lot longer than that. How'd you end up staying out here with them?"

"That's a long story, but the *Reader's Digest* version is that I went to the party with my boyfriend and somebody else left with him. I didn't have any other way to get home, and John asked me to stay. It sounded like fun and I really didn't feel like dealing with Isaac. Then Ricky took me home so I could get some things and clear it with my folks. So, here I am."

"If you want to know the truth," Kate said as she pulled onto the highway, "Ricky sort of scares me."

"He used to scare me too, but after you talk to him for a while, he's really not all that bad. He can be intense sometimes, but what can you expect considering where he comes from?"

"I'm not sure that I know what you mean."

"I probably shouldn't talk about it, but there really are some things you should know if you're going to be hanging around. Ricky's family is pretty messed up. His mom's strung out, and his dad used him to sell drugs and knock him around. That's why he's planning on leaving town and going to school out of state. He wants out and that's his answer."

"It doesn't sound like you're all that happy about that. It sounds to me like getting out would be a good thing."

Shannon started wrapping her hair around her finger. "It is. I just wish he didn't have to skip town to do it. I don't know … it sort of seems like he's running away, and that idea has always bothered me. I've spent months being afraid of him, and when I finally get to know him, it's when he's getting ready to leave. I guess it sort of feels like everyone is trying to leave me behind."

"Do you want him to stay?"

"I don't know. I would sort of like the chance to know him a little better—he's really pretty cool—but I also understand why he wants so bad to get out. When he was taking me home, we had to stop by his house. I stayed out in the car while he went inside. I don't know what went on in there, but when he came out he had that fat lip. I could see in his eyes that he was angry, but it also looked like he wanted to cry."

Kate didn't know what to say. This conversation was going places she hadn't expected. "Have you told him that you want him to stay?"

"What good would that do? Like I said, I hardly know him. I don't think that he's going to go and change his life around just because of what I want. I talked to John a little bit about that this morning, and I guess Ricky has been planning this for a long time."

"I don't know. It just seems to me that he's sort of taken an interest in you. You never know what can happen when you try."

"Girl, there ain't no guy in this world that's ever taken that big of an interest in me, except for my daddy. I thought that Isaac did, but I guess I was just fooling myself about that. I am *not* going to make an idiot of myself like that ever again."

Kate drove quietly as they entered town. She didn't know where to lead the conversation now. She had thought to warn Shannon away from Ricky, but now she wasn't sure if that was what she was supposed to do. Now it was obvious that she didn't know enough about him to make that sort of decision. Kate said a quick prayer for guidance and remained silent until they reached the corner where she was supposed to turn.

"It's funny how conversations move around on you," Shannon said as Kate turned the corner. "We started out talking about how John was driving himself into the poor house and end up talking about me and Ricky. Not that there is a me and Ricky. You know what I mean?"

"Yeah, I know what you mean. I'm sort of glad our conversation ended up like that. I would hate to say something to, or in front of Ricky that I would've regretted. ... Here's the place John was telling me about." Kate pulled into the parking lot of the Roman Manor Pizza Shop. "It looks like an all-right place."

"It looks a lot better than that place where we ate last night, but that was good food. John seems to have a knack for finding places like this. We should see about getting some more sodas as well. There's still plenty of beer back at the house, but I really don't like beer all that much, and the sodas are about gone."

The Roman Manor Pizza Shop turned out to be a fairly new building just off the town square. The inside of the building was decorated to look like classic Roman architecture, but was obviously cheaply done. Otherwise, it was neat and clean and looked like just about any other pizza place either of them had ever seen. A short, middle-aged woman with gray-streaked hair took their order, and the two went to sit on a bench by the door to wait.

"Now, about you and Ricky," Kate said as she made herself comfortable. "I really think that you should talk to him about how the two of you feel. You're not giving him or yourself enough credit. I think he likes you, and that you like him. I also think that if the two of you don't sit down and talk about it, you're both going to regret it for a seriously long time. To be honest, I meant to warn you to stay away from him, but now I don't know if that's the right thing to do. You really need to talk to him."

"Even if I do like him," Shannon replied, "and I guess I do, I don't think that he likes me, at least not that way. If it turns out that we do like each other, I don't know that I would feel right talking to him about that unless he decided on his own to stay, and there's no point in confusing things if he doesn't. I don't know what to do. It seems as though all the options are wrong."

This was the opportunity that Kate had prayed for. Now she knew which direction to take, but she still wasn't sure if it would be a good thing for Shannon to get involved with Ricky, even if he was trying to get his life together. Maybe leaving town really was the best thing for him. There was one sure thing that she could say, however. "Maybe you should pray about it. Maybe you don't know what to do, but God does."

"Now you sound like my grandmother. She's always telling me I need to pray more."

"Maybe your grandmother knows what she's talking about. I don't want to get preachy or anything, but when we rely on ourselves to solve our problems, we usually end up making a bigger mess of things. God is the only one who has all the answers, and his is the only way things will ever turn out right, every time."

"My grandmother is almost always right, that's not in question. I do pray, but not really to God or anything like that. I don't really know if there is a God out there who's listening, but praying does help me sort out my thoughts. In some ways, I don't think I like the idea of somebody else, even if it is God, running my life."

"God doesn't run our lives. He's there to help us when we need him, and personally I need him all the time. Just think about it—what do you really have to lose?"

By the time that Kate and Shannon got back to the farm, everyone else had called it quits for the day. They had cleaned up and were ready to eat the three extra large, supreme pizzas that the girls had picked up. They were all gathered around the table on the back porch eating, drinking, telling stories, and laughing, when they heard someone pull into the driveway around front. Soon, Sheriff Blackwell came around the corner of the wraparound porch.

"What's up, Sheriff?" John said. "Grab yourself a piece of pizza while there's still some left, and make yourself comfortable."

"This isn't a social visit, John. I need to ask a few questions about a young lady named Lisa St. Thomas."

Chapter 9

"Lisa St. Thomas? Do you mean Lyssa? What's she got to do with anything?" Chris asked.

"Lisa, Lyssa, whatever—she was found passed out alongside the road down near the river yesterday morning, and we dragged her car out of the river last night. She'll be all right. Right now she's sitting in county lockup, but she doesn't have much to say. According to her father, she was supposed to be coming out here for your party. What I need to know is, was she here and how long did she stay?"

Chris stared at Sheriff Blackwell for several moments. She wanted to cry, scream, anything, but she couldn't even force herself to breath. Finally, she stood and ran into the house. Sheriff Blackwell started to reach out to stop her, but John reached over and put his hand on the sheriff's arm. "Don't worry about her. I can answer your questions, but I doubt that she could just now."

Sheriff Blackwell thought about it for a moment and reluctantly agreed that John was probably right. He could always talk to her later if he needed to. "Was Miss St. Thomas at your party?"

"She was here for a little while," Ricky told him, "but she didn't stay very long. Maybe an hour at the most."

"Did you talk to her while she was here?"

"No. When I saw her, she was upset about something and on her way out. I don't think she talked to anyone except for Chris," Ricky replied.

"I would imagine that what she was upset about," April said, "was what her brother did to her best friend."

"Who was her best friend, and what did her brother do?"

"Her best friend, maybe her only real friend, was Chris."

"The girl who just ran out of here? Was it Lyssa's brother who attacked her the other day?"

"He's her step-brother, and yeah, that was him," John said. "But there was more to it than that. Chris told me what happened when they were talking. Apparently, they had an argument, and that's why Lyssa took off out of here. She smashed Chris's windshield before she left."

"So, you wouldn't know if she was sober or not when she left?"

"Yes I think she was sober when she left," Kate said. "She was mad, sure, but she seemed sober enough. Do you think the accident was because she was drinking?"

"No, the accident happened because she was stoned out of her mind. She was still stoned when they found her, and the highway patrol found several marijuana cigarettes laced with PCP in her car. They probably won't charge her with anything because they can't place her and the drugs in the car at the same time, but they do want to know where they came from. Did she pick it up here?"

Lee spoke up. "She might have gotten them from somebody at the party, but I don't think so. Like Ricky said, she wasn't here very long and didn't really talk to anyone. Probably, she already had it when she got here."

"Okay, a few more things. Do you know what the argument between Chris and Lyssa was about?"

"I do," John said, "but I don't know that I'd feel comfortable talking about it. It was kind of a personal thing between them. Is that something you really need to know?"

"Probably not, but the HP is going to want to know. I also need to ask if it was possible that she got the drugs from Chris."

Just then, Chris came back outside. "The only thing she got from me was a bottle of bourbon she grabbed on her way out. If you want to know what the argument was about, it was because I kissed her. It really wasn't a big deal, but she flipped out, called me all sorts of names, and left. That's really all there was to it."

"One more thing," Kate said. "If you really want to figure out where the

PCP came from, you might want to talk to her brother, Rich. He's been in trouble before because of it. It wouldn't surprise me if he's the one who gave it to her."

"If he's been in trouble because of drugs before, why wasn't he already locked up?"

"Because his father and his stepfather are both high-priced defense lawyers and his mother is the assistant prosecutor. They've gotten him out of a lot of trouble the past couple of years."

"That's definitely something I need to follow up on then. Thank you, guys, that's all I need for now. I might need to come back later if HP needs anything else. I didn't mean to ruin your night, but that's just the way my day's been. If any of you think of anything else that might be useful, just give me a call. By the way, right now HP is letting me run interference here, but if something serious comes up, that won't last. If there's anything that could connect you to this, I suggest you take care of it. Don't make me regret any of this."

"Thanks for the info, Sheriff. Let us know what happens."

After the sheriff left, they all sat around quietly for some time. Although Lyssa hadn't been all that popular, she had been familiar enough that they were all affected. It was Chris who finally broke the silence. "I almost killed my best friend."

"You had nothing to do with it, Chris," Ricky told her. "If she was messing with angel dust, she did that all on her own. She's a big girl, and she knows better."

"You didn't sell her that stuff, did you Ricky?" April asked.

"No way; you know I never messed with that stuff, no matter what my old man said. I don't know where she got it, but it wasn't from me."

"It just doesn't make any sense," Brad said. "Nearly everything Lyssa does is based on what's best for Lyssa. Why in the world would she go and mess with something that would kill her?"

"It doesn't really matter now, does it?" said Chris. "That's just something I'll have to ask her about whenever she decides she's talking to me again. Look, I need to take a walk. Do you want to go with me, Kate?"

"I'd love to. Brad, could you call my parents and tell them I'll be home just a little later than I thought I would be?"

After getting an agreement from Brad that he would call, Kate followed Chris off the porch and north toward the back of the property. "Are you sure that you want to go this way? It will start to get dark soon."

"Don't worry; we're not going very far. There's a place back here that I want to show you. One of the reasons I asked you to take a walk is that I wanted to come out here and talk, and you're more likely to appreciate this place than anyone else. John showed it to me the first time I visited, but he doesn't really like coming back this way."

"What is it?" Kate asked.

"It's sort of hard to explain. You'll just have to see it. Whenever I want to spend some time alone, I come out here. The building was pretty grimy when I first saw it, but I've spent some time cleaning it up. More work needs to be done, but at least it's a lot better than when I first saw the place."

Chris led Kate over a small hill and down the other side where a spring spilled water into a shallow pool. Just up the hill from the pool was a small stone building built right into the side of the hill. The sun shone through the trees in spots and reflected off the surface of the pool. It was a breath-taking, picture-perfect image.

A stone walkway led the way along the hillside to the door. The oak door itself was in good shape, but the small window in the door was long gone and covered with clear plastic as were the two windows on either side of the door. The stone walls were weathered, and in places, the mortar was beginning to crack. Still, the building looked solid.

The inside of the building was dark. The few small windows all faced away from the sun, and little light filtered through the plastic-covered windows. Chris struck a match and lit a couple of small gas lanterns hanging on either side of the inside of the door. The lanterns gave off just enough light to illuminate what was clearly a small chapel.

It was a small, narrow room with a railed altar at the far end and two wooden benches between the altar and the door. The only other features were a small door off to the side of the altar and a strangely formed cross, with two horizontal bars and the upright bar slightly angled, attached to the wall at the far end. Everything inside was either stone or dark-grained wood.

It was not a beautiful place, but there was about it a sense of comfortable simplicity and an air of ageless peace. "I've never seen a cross like that one," Kate said quietly. "In fact, I don't think I've ever seen anything like this place. It looks like something out of the Middle Ages."

"I told you that it was hard to explain. I wasn't even sure that was a cross. I never could get a straight answer out of John about what this place is. All I know is that I get a sense of peace in here, and I like coming here to think about things. For some reason, when I come in here, none of my problems seem all that important for a little while."

"It seems strange that someone who believes that God has given up on her would spend so much time in a church. Maybe the peace you find when you come here is God's way of telling you that he hasn't given up on you after all."

"Why wouldn't God have given up on me when everyone else has? Well, everyone except for John, I guess, but that's just because he's a sucker for lost causes. That, by the way is what I wanted to talk to you about. I don't know what I'm doing anymore. In just a few days, my life has gone from dreadful to horrible." Chris sat down on one of the benches and turned so that she could rest her crossed legs on it. "It just seems as though there's nothing left. I can't even really talk about it with my closest friends, 'cause I don't really know how I feel. I need something to believe in. I need to believe that God is out there and that he loves me, or at least recognizes that I'm here, but I can't. How could God, or anyone else, love me, when I don't even like myself. The only thing I have in my life that's worth anything is my friends, and I can't stand the idea of getting them even more mixed up in my drama. Even though I want to be with John more than anything else, I can't bring myself to make his life more miserable by my being a part of it. What am I supposed to do?"

Kate sat down next to Chris and reached out to hold her hand. "Letting someone else into your life, Chris, is not going to make them miserable. I don't really know all that much about girls and boys and romance and all that, but I do know that it is easier to bear problems if you don't have to do it alone. It gets even easier if you let God deal with it. God does love you, Chris, even if it doesn't always seem like it. Even if you can't love yourself, God has loved you since before you were born, and he will until the day you die—and beyond that. You just need to believe that and have the faith to love him back."

"I don't have any faith, Kate. I don't even have the faith to believe in nothing. What I do have is the knowledge that whatever I do is going to get all messed up. Anyone who gets close to me is going to end up the same way. How am I supposed to have faith in God?"

"Our whole lives are built on faith, Chris. We couldn't buy things if we didn't have faith that our money was worth something. We couldn't walk if we didn't have the faith to believe that we can. We have faith that the sun is going to come up tomorrow and that the weather forecast is going to be at least partially accurate, and God's predictions have proven to be far more accurate than any weatherman's. You had the faith to believe that I would want to come down here and talk to you, or you wouldn't have asked. You have faith that this place is going to be here, and that it's going to be a peaceful place for you to come and rest. And you have enough faith to believe in God, Chris; you've just forgotten how to turn it on."

"I don't know. I think that might be a little too big of a leap for me. What I really want to know, though, is how do you know that what you believe is real?"

"I know by how I feel when I turn my life over to him, which isn't something you can do once and forget about. It's something you do every day. Sometimes I forget or think that I can do it on my own, and that's when things fall apart. When I pray and let God come in and take care of things, I can feel it. I can feel his presence. Then everything is okay again. The touch of God's hand can't be seen, but it can be felt, and it's very real. All you have to do is pray with conviction for God to come into your life, and he will."

"What do I do if he doesn't want me? The last thing I need is to know for certain that not even God wants me around."

"You said that the only reason John hasn't given up on you is because he's a sucker for lost causes—well, so is God. God isn't going to turn you away. I promise."

"It's been a long time since anybody has promised me anything."

"If you want, I can pray with you right now. We can ask him together."

"I don't think that I'm ready for that yet. There's just way too much happening all at once, and I can't think." Chris stood up and squeezed Kate's hand before letting go. "Thank you for talking to me about all this. I don't know that it's helped all that much just yet, but it means a lot that you'd be willing to come here and talk with me about it."

Kate also stood up and looked into Chris's face. She could see the pain and confusion in her eyes, and maybe just a little bit of hope. "I'm here to talk anytime you need me, but please don't think about it too long. It's not going to get any better unless you let God make it better."

"We'd better get going. It's starting to get dark." Chris extinguished the lanterns and led Kate outside. In the fading light of the setting sun, the two of them made their way back to the house.

Ricky had never been very good at figuring out his emotions. Growing up in a house where emotions were for women and women should be stoned had left him out of touch with all but the most primal of his feelings—anger, fear, and lust. He had never really had friends growing up except for the half-baked children of his parents' full-baked friends. It was not until he met Chris that he began to understand what friendship was supposed to be about.

Since then, with a lot of help from Chris, John, and the others, he had begun to understand that it was all right for a man to express his emotions. The problem was that he didn't always understand what his emotions were. Over the past couple of days, Ricky was beginning to come to terms with another new emotional concept. For several years now, Ricky had believed that he was in love with Chris. Now he was beginning to understand that although he loved Chris, it was not the kind of love he had thought it was. He was beginning to experience feelings even stronger than what he felt for Chris, and he had no idea what to do about them. There was a part of him that wanted to say that he was in love with Shannon, but now more than ever, he realized just how little he understood about that particular feeling. Ricky didn't know if he was in love with her or if what he was feeling was something more or less than love. What he knew was that he wanted to go over and just be with her, hold her hand, and ask her if she felt the same way about him.

He was tempted to scrap the entire idea of leaving for Colorado. He could just stay here and maybe take some time to figure things out. Ricky grabbed his beer off the rail next to him and sulked over to the west side of the porch. He sat on the railing and tried to block everything out and just watch the sun as it began to set. He didn't hear Shannon walk up behind him and was so startled when she sat down on the rail next to him and asked what he was doing that he nearly fell off.

"Sorry, I didn't mean to startle you," Shannon said as she tried to help him wipe off some of the beer he had spilled on his shirt.

"It's not your fault. I just wasn't paying attention. I hadn't really expected anyone to follow me over here."

"It was sort of uncomfortable over there since the only other person I really know here is John, and he went in to take a shower or something. So I thought I'd come over here and see what you were up to."

"Actually, I'm not up to anything. I was just sitting here watching the sun go down. That's not too much excitement for you, is it?"

"I think I'm up to it. It's really pretty out here."

"Yeah, I suppose it is. I'm not really much for the country life, but it's nice to come out here once in a while to get away from things."

"Where do you think Chris and Kate got off to?"

"There's no telling. Most of the time when Chris goes out on her walks, she walks down to the bridge at the end of the road. A couple of times, though, she's walked all the way down to the river. It's generally a waste of time to go look for her, because she usually finds her way back before you can find her. If you hang around long enough, you'll get used to it."

"It's going to be getting dark pretty soon. Do you think they'll be all right?"

"I can't guarantee anything, but Chris knows what she's doing. It's just another day in the sticks."

They sat quietly for a short time, watching the sun, before Shannon worked up the courage to ask her question. "When are you planning to leave?"

"I don't even know anymore. I was planning on leaving around the end of the month, but I might put it off for another month. I think if I had a really good reason to stay, I might just give up the whole idea altogether."

"What about getting away from your family? I thought you wanted to put as much distance as you could between you and your father."

"These guys here are my family. They're the only real family I've ever known. As for my father, well, I'll deal with him when the time comes."

"John said pretty much the same thing this morning. It sounds to me like you've already made up your mind to stay. A couple of days ago, nothing was going to stop you. What brought all this on?"

"I don't know. Cold feet, maybe, or it could be just the reality of what I'd be leaving. Tell me, is your heart set on doing nothing but hanging out here and doing nothing all week?"

"No, not really. I just don't want to go home."

"What do you say we go see a movie, just you and me? I don't know if I'm up to another night of listening to the crickets."

"That sounds good to me. What do you want to go see?"

"I don't really care. We'll just go to the mall and see what's playing. With six theaters, there's got to be something worth watching."

"That'll work, but I think we both need to take showers first. You stink!"

Chapter 10

When Kate and Chris got back to the house, Kate decided to go on home. She was dirty, tired, and smelly. It was never a good sign when you could smell yourself. She felt good about what she had been able to do, though. If nothing else, it seemed as though Chris, at least, was starting to lean in the right direction. The problem was that she hadn't had much of a chance to be alone with Brad all day. He was, after all, the main reason she was even here.

Brad was sitting on the back porch with the others, so she grabbed him by the arm and headed toward her car. "Come on, Brad. Walk me to my car."

As they walked around the house, Brad worked his arm out of Kate's hand and put it around her shoulders. "What were you and Chris talking about?"

"If you think about it, you could probably figure it out." It felt good to have Brad's arm around her. She moved in a little closer to him as they walked. "She's a little tense right now. Considering how her week's gone, I think Chris is holding up pretty well. She sure is stuck on John, though."

"Yeah, well, those two deserve each other. I'm pretty sure that they're both stuck with each other, but they're also both too scared to admit it. It's the weirdest thing I've ever seen. Neither one of them is shy until they get together."

When they got to where Kate had parked her tan Road Runner, she turned so that she could lean against the front of the car and face Brad. As his arm fell off her shoulder, she took his hand and squeezed it slightly. "What about us, Brad? What are we doing? Am I officially your girlfriend now, or are we just playing around? I really need to know."

"It's not really official, yet. I was sort of hoping to take care of that tomorrow. We're not just playing around, though. I've never been more serious about anything in my life. The problem is that I don't know what to do about it."

"What do you mean you don't know what to do about it? You ask me to be your girlfriend, I say yes, we kiss, and then it's official. It sounds pretty simple to me."

"Yeah, I got that part figured out. That's not really what I'm talking about. What I mean is, half the time, I'm afraid to touch you. I don't know if I'm supposed to touch you. I don't know how I'm supposed to touch you. I don't want to do something wrong and get you mad at me."

"It's not really all that complicated, Brad. I'm not really any different from any other girl. I want you to hold my hand, and I want you to hug me and kiss me. Now, if you want to go any further than that, you're going to have to wait. It's going to require a *serious* commitment to go that far."

"I can live with that," Brad said.

"So, what did you mean when you said you were going to make it official tomorrow?"

"It's a surprise. You'll find out in the morning. When you come back in the morning, you need to bring a change of clothes. We're going to have a cook-out tomorrow, and then we're just going to hang out and listen to some tunes or tell ghost stories or something. Then you can preach to my friends some more."

"That's not what I've been doing, and you know it. I've just been talking to them. I just want to help, and that's how I do that. Does it bother you?"

"No, it doesn't bother me. I was just kidding. Actually, I kind of admire you for it. I don't think that I could talk like that to people I barely know. One of the things I like about you is that I always know where you're coming from. There's no false advertisement so to speak."

"Thank you. It helps to know you feel that way. You know, it wouldn't hurt you to try praying every so often. It's habit forming, but it's one habit you can live with."

"Don't get in such a hurry; you've got a long time to work on me. One more thing, while I'm thinking about it. What's your favorite song?"

"Why do you want to know that?"

"I just want to know. It's just another way I can get to know you a little better."

"I guess. Do you promise not to laugh if I tell you?"

"Why would I do that? Sure, I promise not to laugh."

"Well, my favorite song is 'Crazy Train.'"

"'Crazy Train'? By Ozzy?" Brad laughed.

"You promised that you wouldn't laugh."

"I'm sorry," Brad said. "You just caught me off guard. I expected you to say something like 'Rock of Ages' or 'Amazing Grace.' Probably the last thing I would have expected is Ozzy."

"It's not really Ozzy that I like," Kate replied. "I just like the music. It drives my parents crazy, but I love that kind of guitar music, and Randy Rhoads was about the best."

"I bet it does drive your parents crazy. Do you listen to that a lot at home?"

"Not a lot, really. I have some other music that's almost as good that they're okay with. I do have a big poster of Randy on my wall, though."

Brad chuckled. "That's just crazy. Hey, I learned something new about you, so I guess that makes it a good day."

Brad gave her a kiss, and they said good night. As she drove home, Kate felt better than she could ever remember feeling before. She wasn't sure if she felt this way because she had been doing what God wanted her to, or if it was because of Brad. She suspected that it was both. One thing she knew for sure was that she never wanted to lose this feeling. She also knew that she wanted to share the feeling so that others could experience the same joy.

John was sitting in the living room talking to Lee and April when Chris came back from her walk with Kate. He started to say something to her, but she went straight upstairs without talking to anyone and got into the shower. While she was in the bathrooms, everyone else left. Ricky and Shannon went to find a movie, Lee and April decided that they should do something as a couple, and Brad said something about running some errands and checking in on his sisters. That left just John and Chris in the house.

When she finally came down, she was dressed in a set of baggy, blue sweats. Her hair was still damp and hung in long, heavy curls around her face. "Where is everybody?"

Even though it bothered John to see the pain and fear in Chris's eyes, he could not keep his eyes off her face. "Kate went home, and everybody else found something they had to do elsewhere. I don't think they're quite ready for this quiet country life."

"There's nothing quiet about this house, John. Even when nobody's here, it creaks and moans constantly. I have a question for you, and I want you to be absolutely honest with me. Just forget about us being friends for a few seconds. Can you do that?"

"I don't know if I can, but I'll try. What's up?"

"John, do you think I'm a lost cause?"

"A lost cause? No. I mean, your life is pretty messed up, I know that, but that doesn't make you a lost cause. Think about what you've done. Where would Ricky be if you hadn't come along? Finding you the right guy is April's life work, now that she's got Brad all hooked up. Without you, Lyssa would have been nothing more than a pathetic, lonely girl. You've been a friend to anybody who's really needed one. If there's one person around here that isn't a lost cause, it's you."

"You didn't spend much time thinking over your answer. Are you sure that it wasn't friendship talking?"

"I don't have to think about it, Chris. That answer was as plain as daylight. Do you know how many hours a day I spend thinking about you, and everything you've done for me, and what you mean to me? There are times when I can't think about anything else. No one could know better than me what it's worth to have you around. I'm not the only one who knows it either. Everyone around here knows how special you are, except for you." John brought himself up short. He had gotten carried away and said things he hadn't meant to. "I'm sorry, Chris. I didn't mean to bring all that up. You probably don't want to hear about how often I'm thinking of you."

"It's okay, John. I've suspected for some time how you felt. I just don't think I could bear the thought of pulling you any deeper into this mess that I call my life. It doesn't upset me that you think about me either. There's no comparison between you and Rich Perry. There was one positive thing that came out of what happened. Would you believe that my uncle apologized to me?"

"I guess that's something, anyway. Did it really help, though?"

"Strangely enough, it did. I mean, it doesn't undo everything that he did to me over the years, but it shows me that there's at least some hope. I have another question for you that may seem out of place, but it's really important to me. Do you believe in God, John?"

That was one question John was unprepared for. "I used to believe in God, but I really don't know anymore. When I was young, my mother took me to Sunday school every week, and I would sit there and listen. I believed the things they said back then. When my mother died, though, I lost interest. My step dad used to try and get me to go with him, but eventually, he stopped going too. When you're twelve years old, you just aren't prepared to deal with that sort of loss. When my grandfather died after that, I guess I sort of lost faith in the idea of a loving God."

Chris got up from the chair she was sitting in and came over to sit next to John on the couch. "I haven't exactly found a lot of reasons to put much faith in the idea myself. Right now I'm finding it even harder to see some sort of purpose in life. I mean, what's the point in waking up tomorrow? I need something to believe in. There has to be something that gives some sort of value to just going on."

"Is that what you were talking about with Kate?"

"Sort of, but this didn't start with her. I've just never had anyone to talk with about it before. I used to watch those guys on TV, you know, Jimmy Baker and Jimmy Swaggart and some of the others, and a lot of what they said sounded good. Sometimes, I could almost believe, but it's hard to put that kind of trust in the words of someone who's just a picture on a small screen. They can't answer your questions, and the one time I tried going to a local church, I was asked to leave. So when I got the opportunity to talk to someone who might have the answer and was willing to spend the time with me, I had to take advantage of it. Even if she's wrong about God, she's got the answers to something. More than anything, I want my life to be like hers."

"I have to admit, Kate does seem like she's got it together. I wish I had the answers you're looking for, but I don't. So if you think that she might have the answers you need, then you should do what you can to get them from her. Whatever you decide to do, I'll support you."

"You know, I took her down to that little chapel down by the spring. It's always a good place for me to go and think through things. For just a moment, while we were talking, there was this really warm feeling I got. It was almost like somebody was holding me. I decided I have to find out, John. If there's anything at all to the things that Kate believes, then it's got to be better than fumbling through life the way I am now. I'm really glad you understand. Having you here is the only thing that has kept me from going crazy the past couple of days. Maybe, when I get myself straightened out, we can talk about if there's some kind of future for us."

"Well, now I really wish I had some answers for you. Not to change the subject or anything, but since it's just the two of us here, I've got a surprise for you. I don't want you to read too much into it, though. It's just a gift from a friend who's concerned about you."

"What kind of gift?"

John stood up and grabbed Chris's hand to pull her up. "Come on, I'll show it to you. It's out in the garage."

With both her curiosity and suspicion aroused, Chris followed as John led her outside by the hand. It was the first time John had touched her in days, and Chris really liked the way it felt. The garage was really nothing more than a small barn, connected to the house by a breezeway. John had kept it locked up for over a week now, and nobody had been able to get in. There was a small door in the side with a padlock, and two big doors in front that locked from the inside.

John opened the padlock and hung it on a nail beside the doorway. He led her inside and turned on the lights only when she was through the door. John studied her face intently as she first laid eyes on the little red Mercury.

For the first time in days, he liked what he saw there. He took the keys out of his pocket and handed them to her. "So, what do you think? I saw it and thought of you immediately."

"It's beautiful, John, but I can't take this from you. This is way too much."

"It's too late. I already had it titled in your name. It really wasn't all that much. I picked it up pretty cheap. You need a new car, and right now, there's no way you can afford one on your own. I saw the car, I had the money, and I bought it for you. It bothered me that you were driving that old Rambler. The brakes on it are worthless, and it keeps breaking down on you. Not to mention the fact that right now it doesn't have a windshield. I don't want you to feel obligated to me or anything. I just want to be sure that you can get out here to see me once in a while, safely. This one isn't exactly new, but it is in better shape than what you're driving now. I've had it for about a week now. I didn't want to embarrass you or anything either, which is why I wanted to give it to you when it was just the two of us."

"I don't know what to say, John. Thank you!"

"That's all you need to say. Why don't you get in and take it for a drive? See what you think of it."

John opened the garage doors as Chris got in and started the car. She backed out until the driver's window was about even with where John was standing. "Do you want to go with me?"

"No, you go ahead. I think I'm going to stay here and read for a while, and then I'm probably going to crash. I have to go into town first thing in the morning to drop some stuff off at work. Have fun, and I'll see you later."

John closed the garage doors as Chris pulled out of the driveway. He was aware that there was no way a car was going to make Chris's problems go away, but it was good to see a smile on her face, even if was just temporary. He watched as she drove off. She didn't exactly spin her wheels as she left, but she was definitely in a hurry to get out on the road. When he couldn't see her taillights anymore, he turned and walked back up to the house. Inside, he put on some reading music and sat down to read a book. It had been a long day, and the emotional stress of the past week caught up with him early. John read only a couple of pages before falling asleep to the music of Mendelssohn.

Shock was the only word that Chris could think of to describe the way she was feeling. She had been more than a little suspicious when John led her out to the garage to reveal his surprise, but she never expected that he would buy her a car. John said that he had gotten it cheap, but she knew him well enough to know that he probably wasn't being completely honest about that. As much as she wanted to give it back, though, she really liked it. She also didn't know how she would be able to get him to take it back. Chris felt guilty for even driving the car, but grateful to have a friend like John. If there was a God, then she was certain that John was his gift to her.

When she got home, Kate said hello to her parents and went down the hall to take a shower. Afterward, she felt much better with all the grime gone. She had intended to go straight to bed, but now that she was clean, she didn't feel all that tired. Besides, she wanted to talk with her parents about all the things that had happened.

She was beginning to think that Chris was the key to the whole group. John would probably tag along wherever Chris went, and between the two of them, they seemed to have a great deal of influence with Ricky. April would most likely tag along as well, if for no other reason than to not be left behind. Lee was friendly, but he tried to avoid her as much as possible. Shannon seemed receptive enough, but Kate didn't know what would be needed to push her definitively towards God. The first step, she decided, was to get Chris going in the right direction. Kate felt sort of guilty for being so analytical about everything, when there were good people suffering needlessly, but somehow, that just seemed to be the best way to work on them.

Kate walked into the living room, where her parents were both reading, and sat down on the couch. "I had quite a day today. I think it turned out all right, though."

"So, what happened? Did you get a chance to talk to them?" her mom asked.

"Well, not all of them, but I got to talk to some of them, anyway. I also got a chance to see one of the most beautiful little chapels I've ever seen. It wasn't all good, though. Do you know Lyssa St. Thomas?"

"Sure," her father said, "that's Jack St. Thomas's daughter. I don't really know the family very well, but I've worked with Jack on several things. Why, what happened?"

"We found out that she was in an accident a couple of days ago."

"Dear Lord," her mother said, "let her be all right."

"She's okay, I guess, but she was arrested for possession after she ran her car off the road. The sheriff came around asking some questions about her; I guess she was pretty good friends with Chris. To be honest, I never really paid all that much attention to her. I always thought she was kind of annoying." That confession carried a pang of guilt with it.

"How did your friends take it?"

"Well, Chris took it pretty hard, but the others seemed to take it like any other bad news. I get the feeling they weren't all that fond of her either. It's a shame, because she really didn't have that many friends. I wish now that I had tried to spend more time with her, maybe talk to her some more."

"You can't go back and change that now. Who knows, you might get a chance to talk to her again soon, but you can't save everyone. All you can really do is concentrate on those you can help, and it seems to me that these new friends of yours could definitely use whatever help you can give them. Did you get very far with any of them?"

"As a matter of fact, it kind of surprised me, but Chris came to me after we ate and asked me to take a walk with her. That's what I really wanted to talk about. We walked down to the spring, where someone had built this little chapel, and she started asking me about God. She really wants to believe, I think, but for some reason, she just kept holding back. I could hear the pain and fear and desperation in her voice. I wanted to pray with her so bad, but she said that she wasn't really ready. I'm going to try and talk to her again tomorrow. The others all seemed willing to talk to me, except for Lee, but none of them seem to be anywhere close to being as ready to make a decision the way Chris was. I think that if I can just get Chris to make that decision, it might be easier to convince the rest of them. She seems to be the common denominator."

"I wouldn't take that for granted if I were you," her mom said, "but you do need to keep working on her. Also, keep in mind that you're not the one that's going to get her to make that decision, Jesus is. If she's as close as you seem to think she is, though, then you can't afford to not do whatever you need to do as soon as possible. What about Brad, did you get a chance to talk with him much?"

"Not nearly as much as I would have liked. We were pretty busy all day, and then all that stuff with Lyssa came up. I didn't get a chance to talk with him until just before I left. We managed to get a few things worked out. When I tried to talk to him about praying, though, he told me not to get in such a hurry. He said that he was going to be around for a while and that there was plenty of time to work on him."

"Speaking of not getting in a hurry," her mother said, "I wanted to talk to you about that. Brad seems to be a nice enough guy, but do you think he's going to respect your decision to wait?"

"That's one of the things that we talked about, Mom. I told him very plainly that he would have to wait, and he said that he could live with that. He also told me that he respected me for being firm in my decisions. I was sort of worried about that as well, but for now at least, it's a settled matter."

"Well, I'm glad to hear that. I take it that you're going back out there tomorrow?"

"Yeah, we're going to do some more painting, and then we're going to have a cookout. I might be late again tomorrow."

"That's fine, sweetheart, just as long as we know where you are. Did you think to get the phone number for us?"

"Yes, I did. It's in my purse. Remind me to give it to you in the morning before I leave. Right now, I think I'm going to bed. It's been a long day, and tomorrow looks like it's going to be just as long."

Kate said good night to her parents and went to her room. She picked out some clothes to work in tomorrow as well as a change for later. Then she sat down at her desk to say her evening prayers. Kate briefly considered kneeling beside her bed, but she hadn't done that since she was a kid and wasn't sure she would be all that comfortable doing it now.

She would never be able to remember the words she prayed. She would never forget, however, the intense power that surged through her as she released herself to the will of God. Kate brought to her prayers a new conviction and a belief in what she was doing that she had never before known. The result was that she could feel herself being submersed in the will of God.

Losing all sense of herself and of time, she gave herself over to communion. When at last she closed her prayer, she found herself sitting on the floor with tears of joy streaming down her face. Even as she climbed into bed and fell asleep, she felt the presence of God as he watched over her slumber.

Chapter 11

John woke up when Brad came in, but only long enough to move upstairs to his bed. When his alarm went off at 5:00, he felt much better than he would have imagined. He hadn't even bothered to change clothes before he crashed, which was beginning to be a source of some discomfort. He went over to the window to see what the day had to offer. It was dark, but the sun was beginning to come up. There were more clouds in the sky, but it still promised to be a beautiful day.

He turned from the window and reached for his cigarettes on the table next to the bed. Instead, he found a card that had been left there sometime during the night. He pulled the card out of the envelope to find that it was a simple blue card with big yellow letters saying "THANK YOU." Inside was a note written in Chris's neat script.

> John,
>
> I can't say enough to thank you for the car. I still do not think that I should accept it, but I know you well enough to know that you would never let me give it back. I don't think I could ever find the words to explain how much it means to me to know that you care about me the way you do. I've never been very good at putting things into writing, but I had to do something to let you know that I appreciate everything you've done for me. You're the best friend that I could ever hope to

find, and I hope to be able to return all the favors someday.

Love,
Chris

John put the card back into the envelope, and then he placed it in a box that he kept on his dresser for such things. As soon as he changed his clothes, he grabbed his keys and went downstairs. He briefly considered putting a pot of coffee on but didn't want to wait for it to brew; he just wanted to drop the plates off at the print shop and get back as soon as he could.

It was an uneventful trip, and when he got back, John found the rest gathered by the gate where Chris was showing off her new car. He parked in front of the garage and walked over to where they were standing.

"It's about time you got back," Brad said. "We were all getting ready to hop in this hot rod and leave you. Actually, I figured you were still asleep until I came out here and saw your car was gone. Dude, you crashed hard last night."

"Yeah, I wanted to get some reading done last night, but I don't think I got through a whole page."

"It was that music that you were listening to when I came in. I've been telling you that stuff is snooze city. Now, if you'd had some AC/DC or something playing, you'd have been all right."

"Maybe, but you can't read when you're listening to AC/DC. The whole point was to relax, and I certainly did that."

Ricky came up next to him and put his hand on John's shoulder. "I got a question for you, John. How come you didn't buy the rest of us a car?"

"Because the rest of you already have cars that are in better shape than mine. You guys are on your own. Besides, you don't look as good when you get excited."

Ricky laughed. "I'll have to give you that last point." Ricky walked back around to stand next to Shannon. John noticed that he was holding Shannon's hand.

"I don't suppose that either of you is going to tell me what went on between the two of you last night."

Shannon's face turned red, and she looked at Ricky. "Let's just say that we worked out an agreement that was appealing to both of us. The rest is none of your dang business."

"It looks like everyone around here is getting hooked up except me and Chris."

Although John meant it as a joke, April's reply was very serious. "I guess we could leave the two of you alone again, and you could take care of that. Maybe this time you'll get it right."

"I think this conversation is going nowhere," Chris told them. "I think we need to find something else to talk about."

"What are we working on today, John?" Lee asked. "I think we got all the painting done yesterday, right?"

"Yeah, the painting's done. I think the only thing left to do to the house is to put the shutters back up. Other than that, I think we're done."

Chris leaned back against the car and drained a cold cup of coffee. "We still haven't cleaned out the barn from the party. I think I'll work on that. There ain't no way you're going to get me up on a ladder. I can do enough damage to myself by falling off the ground."

Just then, Kate pulled into the yard and got out of her car. "Good morning, everyone. So, what's going on today?"

"You have a choice: you can either go hold a ladder for these here he-men so they can put up shutters, or you can give me a hand cleaning out the barn. I'll warn you though, with these guys, you'd probably be better off well away from potential falling objects."

John lightly punched Brad in the arm. "Brad, I find it comforting to know that the ladies have so much confidence in us. Do you think we could ever possibly live up to their high expectations?"

"Considering we dropped every one of those things when we took them down, I don't think there will be any problem with that. I know that I'm going to be at the top of the ladder, not the bottom."

"Oh, ye of little faith. I've got it all figured out. If you're lucky, I might let you in on my little secret. Now, I can't make any promises on screws or tools, but I think I can keep the shutters from crashing down on top of anybody."

"If it's all the same to you," Chris said, "I still think I'm going to hide out in the barn."

"I'm thinking Chris is pretty smart," Kate said, "and that I'll hide out in the barn with her."

Putting the shutters back up proved to be a great deal more difficult than taking them down. Since none of them had any real experience doing that kind of work, it also took a lot more time than it should have. Despite all the swearing, sweating, and bloody knuckles, however, they did manage to get the shutters all back in place without dropping any of them. They also had a lot more fun than they were willing to admit. Even though it was John's house, they all thought of it as home, and there was always an advantage to working together with friends on a project that everyone cared about. Of course, there was nothing wrong with a little friendly competition to see who could get the most done either.

In the barn, Chris and Kate used large push brooms and a snow shovel to clean up. They had the doors and windows open to air out the pungent aroma of stale beer and cigarette smoke. Kate dumped a load of trash into a metal container. "You know, Chris, a person could almost get drunk just from the smell in here."

"It is pretty bad, isn't it," Chris replied. "We really should have done this a couple of days ago, but I don't think anyone wanted to think about it. It's not as bad as I was afraid it was going to be, though."

"What is John going to do with all this?"

"There's a small landfill all the way in the back of the property along the fence line that John shares with the sheriff. The only thing he can't dump back there are paint cans and stuff with a lot of chemicals in it. That container fits on that trailer hooked up behind the riding mower."

"So, have you thought any about what we talked about yesterday?"

"Actually, it's almost the only thing I have been thinking of. In fact, I have another question for you. It may sound strange, but the idea keeps nagging at the back of my mind. Do you think it's possible that God put John in my life for a reason?"

"I'm not sure I understand what you mean."

"I mean, I know he's not a Christian or anything, and he's certainly no saint, but I think that he just might be the best person I know. He's generous, caring, self-sacrificing, and no matter what, he can always find a way to make me feel better. He's always looking out for other people, even the ones who don't like him. I mean, Lyssa and John couldn't stand each other, but while Lyssa was always polite, John was really nice to her. Or take Shannon for example, even though he only knows her from work, and not really for very long, he invites her to come stay with us just because she wants to get away from her ex-boyfriend for a while. I'm not very good at explaining things, but it just seems to me that John is what most Christians claim to be. Am I making any sense?"

"Yeah, I think I know what you're getting at, and you're right, John is a great guy. I've never met anyone quite like him before. I also think you're right on, there's no doubt in my mind that there's a reason God brought the two of you together. God is always looking out for us, even when we're not paying attention. Of course, it could be that your opinion of him is slightly biased."

Chris pushed another pile of hay and trash into the shovel that Kate held. "There's that too, I guess. I think though, that the reason I like him is because of the things I see in him rather than I'm seeing these things because I like him. Anyway, it's just an idea that I had, but it's one that won't go away. I like to think that it's true, and I *really* want it to be, but I don't have any experience with this. I don't know how much of what I'm thinking is true and how much is wishful thinking."

"You probably understand more than what you're giving yourself credit for. It's also possible that you're God's gift to John. God has a plan for both of you. What those plans might be and if they include both of you together in the long term, I have no idea. I do know that he brought you together for a reason, and whatever that reason is, it's going to be good for both of you."

"Last night, I talked some with John about the conversation we had. I was sort of nervous because I wasn't sure what he would think about it. I've never heard him talk about things like God and church. I don't really know what I expected, but I was sort of surprised by where he was at. I felt a lot better after I talked to him, though. It seemed like he understood where I was coming from, and he told me he'd support me in whatever decision I made."

"Is that what was holding you back yesterday?"

"Mostly. No matter what happens, I don't think I could stand to lose John. I don't want you to think that I'm more interested in a guy than I am in God. It's just that having John around makes it easier to believe in God—if that makes any sense."

"It does, but you need to be careful. If you let yourself get so focused on John and his opinion, no matter what that opinion is, it's going to get really difficult for you to hear the things God has to say. That's true no matter who you're talking about. You said that it was mostly John who was holding you back. What else is bothering you?"

Chris leaned against a pole and shook her head slightly. "I guess the rest of it is just me getting in my own way. You said that God loves me, but I don't see it. How could God love someone like me?"

"How could he not love you, Chris? He's your father and you're his child. Of course he loves you."

"My father loved me so much he shot himself. My uncle loved me so much he used to jump in my bed at night. My mother loves me so much she kicked me out of the house. The truth is that I'm not that lovable. I'm not a good person, and I don't deserve to be loved by my parents, John, or God."

"You're right, but you're also wrong. None of us deserve God's love, that's what makes it so awesome to know that he loves us anyway. That's the miracle that's proven by Jesus' sacrifice. Tell me, what do you know about the crucifixion?"

"Only that Jesus was hung on a cross to die. I've never really understood why that's so important."

"The reason it's so important," Kate told her, "is that the Romans only crucified the very worst criminals that way. By dying on the cross, Jesus paid the penalty for even the worst of our crimes so that we could be free to just accept the love he has for us. There's nothing you could have done that's so bad that the cross won't cover it."

"That sounds good, Kate, but I know myself. I know what I've done right and what I've done wrong. If I know all that, then I'm sure God does also."

"You know, Jesus wasn't crucified by himself. There were two other men who were executed with him. The Bible says that they were thieves, but I don't think that we really understand what that means. Like I said, the Romans only crucified the very worst criminals, so these guys weren't there for purse snatching or shoplifting. These guys were the very worst that the Roman Empire had to offer. These were bad guys.

"Anyway, the book of Luke tells us that one of the thieves mocked Jesus from his cross. The other thief, though, confessed Jesus as his Savior and asked Jesus to forgive him. Jesus' reply was that they would be together in heaven that very day. Even now, that man is sitting at the foot of God basking in his love. If God can love and forgive that thief, then I know that God loves you."

"You know, I've heard that story before, but no one ever explained it before. Okay, one more question. Why is it so important to you that I become a Christian?"

Kate sat down on a stool next to where Chris was. "Remember what I said about the feel of God's touch? It is such an incredible experience that there is no way that I could ever describe it to you, and there's a joy that goes with it that is unlike anything you've ever experienced.

"Last night, I was thinking about you and John and Brad and everyone, and I prayed for guidance so that I could do what he wanted me to. As I was praying, I just let myself go entirely. I just turned everything over to God. I've got to tell you that I've never experienced anything like that before. Afterwards, I thought about how great it would be if I could share that feeling with you. It's there, Chris; all you have to do is ask for it. Over the past couple of days, I've come to think of you as a good friend, and I want to share this with you. That's the sort of thing that friends do."

"Careful, you've only seen the very tip of this disaster. You start calling me your friend, and you're likely to hear all about it."

"That's all right. That's what I want. Anytime you want to talk, all you have to do call me."

Just then, Brad walked through the door. "I should've known I'd find the two of you in here flappin' your jaws. Here we are, out there breaking our backs, working like dogs, and the two of you are in here having a nice little chat."

"It's not our fault that you aren't smart enough to hide out in here with us," Chris told him. "Work is one of them four-letter words that I try to avoid whenever I can."

"Come on, we're going to take a break for lunch, and we need the womenfolk to fix it for us."

Chris looked at Kate and raised her eyebrow. "There are times when I would like to fix him some lunch, seasoned with something to seal that mouth of his. It would make life easier around here if he couldn't talk quite so much."

"Yeah, but then he would just find some other way of making our lives miserable."

"If I couldn't talk, you'd all die of boredom, 'cause then you'd have nothing left to complain about. Actually, Lee and April picked up some lunch meat and Kaiser rolls last night, and we're going to make some subs. So it's everyone for themselves—if you want some, you'd better get to it before Ricky does."

Chris straightened herself out and dusted off. "He's got a point there. If we don't get to the food before Ricky, there's not likely to be anything left. That boy can eat like nothing you've ever see."

"I guess we'd better get going then," Kate said. "Ricky's a lot closer to the food than we are."

※

Lunch was simple, but it was enough to satisfy everyone, except for Ricky who started complaining as soon as the food ran out. After they ate, they sat around for a time talking about the morning's work and what still needed to be done. At some point during the conversation, Brad and Kate managed to slip off by themselves. Brad led Kate by the hand upstairs to his room. "I told you that I was going to make this official today, and this is as good a time as any."

Brad had Kate sit on the end of one of the beds and went over to the dresser next to the window. He pulled a small cardboard box from the top drawer and handed it to her. "I never bothered with a class ring or anything, so I had to think of something else to give you to wear." Brad watched as she opened the box and pulled out a thin gold chain with a heart pendant. "I don't know if it's worth anything, but it belonged to my grandmother. I don't have the money to spend on something expensive, but I don't think I could have found anything more appropriate if I did. I hope you'll wear it as a sign of how much you mean to me. I know it's not much, but it's all I have."

Kate held the necklace so that the small medallion sat in the palm of her hand. The pendant was a gold heart with a cross inset. "It's beautiful, Brad. I don't need anything expensive. It means a lot that you would give me something that belonged to your grandmother. But are you really sure that you want to give this to me?"

"Yes, I'm sure. I don't know anyone that this would be more appropriate for. It's not really anything special. I think it's just a trinket that my grandfather gave her when they were young. It's been sitting in that box for years. My grandmother gave it to me before she died and said that I should give it to a girl who was really special. I think it would make her happy to know that girl is you."

"In that case, I'll wear it proudly. Could you help me put it on?"

Kate turned away from Brad and held up her hair so that he could fasten the chain together. Once it was secure, Kate went over to a mirror. One look at it around her neck and her eyes began to tear up, and she turned to hug Brad fiercely. "Thank you, Brad. Thank you very much. You've made me so happy."

Brad returned the hug. He was as happy as he could ever remember being.

Downstairs, John, Ricky, and Lee had gone out to check on the supplies for the fire, leaving Chris, April, and Shannon alone in the kitchen. April got a soda from the refrigerator and sat down at the table. "So, tell me this, Chris, what have you and Kate been talking about the past two days?"

"A lot of things, really, but mostly I've been asking about her church and stuff like that."

April took a long drink and set her soda on the table. "Are you really interested in that or is she just preaching at you?"

"No, I really want to know. I just can't seem to get anything else to make sense anymore, so I thought I'd see what she had to say. I figure if Kate's right, then I need to look into it some more. If she's not right, then I guess I really haven't lost anything. Either way, though, I feel I need to find out for sure."

Shannon tossed her empty can into the trash can. "I don't know how much God has to do with it, but I've noticed that around my neighborhood, people like my parents, who go to church regularly, seem to be a lot better off than those that don't."

"What do you mean?" April asked.

"Well, take Isaac's folks for example. At least twice a week, the police are down there 'cause his old man's beating up on his mom. I don't think my dad's ever even raised his voice to my mom. A lot of the people at my parents' church have been married for years, where a lot of folks who don't go have been married three or four times. I don't go to church much, myself, but my mom and dad always seem to be holding hands when they come home after services. Like I said, I don't know if it's God or just the atmosphere there, but I definitely think that there's something in the church that helps people."

Chris sat back in her chair and played with a butter knife. "I don't know anyone who goes to church. Everyone in my uncle's neighborhood pretty much keeps to themselves. Even the kids around there don't really play together all that much. It's not exactly a social hot spot of the greater metropolitan area, if you know what I mean. That's why I've hardly ever been to church. The one time I did go, I think they knew my uncle, so they weren't exactly friendly to me."

"I don't know that you're really missing all that much," April told her.

"As far as I've ever been able to tell, it's just a building. I go with my parents sometimes, mostly on Christmas and Easter, and for the most part they just sing songs and tell stories. Then the preacher gets up, tells everyone that they're all sinners, asks them for money, and everyone goes home. The next week, nobody can even remember your name. I believe in God, but I don't think he spends a lot of time in church."

"You may be right," Chris replied, "but I think I need to find out for myself. I was thinking about asking Kate if I could go with her tomorrow morning."

"Well, you go right ahead and do that," April told her as she picked up her soda. "I think that I'm going to sleep late tomorrow. I plan on having a really good time tonight and being up late, and that means sleeping in."

Just then, the guys came back in. "Are you girls about ready to get back to work?" John asked. "We only have two more windows to do, and Lee is going to get the grill started for the barbecue. Where's Brad and Kate?"

"I think they went upstairs," April answered. "I haven't seen them since we finished lunch. I think Brad was getting jealous of all the time Kate was spending with Chris."

Lee picked up the bag of charcoal, which was sitting on the floor next to the counter. "Maybe she's praying for him. I'm sure she needs something to fill up all those spare moments."

Ricky held the door open for him. "Be nice, Lee. She ain't any more odd than the rest of us."

"I have been nice. Mostly, though, I've just avoided her. If she starts preaching at me, I'm going to tell her to buzz off. I don't want to hear any of that nonsense."

"I'll go see what they're doing," Chris said as she got up from the table. "I need to use the girls' room anyway."

Chris ran into Brad and Kate as they were coming down the stairs. "There you guys are. Are you ready to get back to work?" Chris didn't wait for either of them to answer, because it was then that she noticed the necklace Kate was wearing. "Oh my, Kate, did he give you that?"

"Yes, to both questions."

Chris leaned back against the railing. "I guess this thing with you two is pretty serious then. Congratulations, guys, I'm really happy for both of you."

Brad looked both proud and embarrassed. "Thanks. … Are they down in the kitchen or already outside?"

"They were heading out when I came this way, but you know how that goes. They're probably still in the kitchen arguing over who's going to get the most done. I told them I'd come and get you."

"Well then," Kate said as she continued down the stairs, "I suggest that we get back to work so we can get on with the feast."

"I'll be out in a few," Chris replied. "Nature's calling."

Chris went on up the stairs to the bathroom and closed the door behind her. She stared at herself in the mirror for several long moments. She understood that things change, but she could not understand why so many things had to change at once. She really was very happy for both Kate and Brad, but Brad having a girlfriend was the final blow to the world that Chris knew a week ago. It seemed as though Ricky had finally gotten himself a girlfriend, Brad was now officially connected to Kate, and by the end of the summer, many of her friends would be spread out across the country. Lee was joining the Marines, April was going to school at State, Ricky was leaving for Colorado, and God only knows where she would end up.

Only John was the same as he had always been, but how long would he be satisfied with a promise? Sooner or later he was going to get tired of waiting for her to make up her mind, and then he too would be gone for good. As Chris studied her image in the mirror, she could see the changes in herself as well. She had always spent at least an hour every day fixing her hair, but now it just hung loosely around her face. The large shirt she wore hung loosely from her shoulders, hiding the fact that she was female. The biggest change though, was in her eyes. There were large, dark circles around her eyes from the lack of sleep, and the eyes themselves had a glassy, distant look to them. She looked like someone raised in the wild.

Chris could not remember a time when she did not long for changes in her life. Now that things were changing, she found herself unprepared. What other changes did the world have in store for her? Only time, and maybe God, would have the answer for that. "God, I don't know if you're listening, or if you even want to hear from me. I've never done this before, so I don't know if I'll get it right, but if you are listening, I could really use some help here. I have to make some decisions, and I don't think that I have the strength to make them, or the brains to make the right ones. If there's anything you can do for me, I'd really appreciate all the help I could get. Thanks."

The rest of the work went quickly, and almost before he knew it, John found himself looking at his house, finished at last. There were still a lot of little things to be done, but all the major repairs were now finished. It didn't look exactly like he remembered it, but it sure was pretty. John was only vaguely aware of the fact that Kate was standing next to him until she spoke. "It sure is a nice place. Is it what you were hoping for?"

"It's a lot more than that, Kate. It's a whole lot more. I guess you could say that this place is a monument to my family. My stepdad is a good guy, but he's never really been family to me. The family that I knew came from this house, so I'm really glad to get it all fixed up."

"You're a lucky guy to have friends who would put this much work into helping you. I don't think that I've ever met a group of people like you guys before."

"Sure you have. You've just never run across them all gathered in one place like this before. We were just able to all get together, that's all. Most people like us end up without a lot of real friends."

"I'm not sure I understand what you mean."

"Well, you know that there are all sorts of cliques out there. You have your jocks, rockers, preps, freaks, and even the nerds have their own little group. For the people in those cliques, all of the people in that group are their friends, and all the people outside that group are 'other people.' That's who we are—'other people.' None of us have ever been able to really fit in anywhere and have been generally excluded, so we got together and made our own little clique so we could fit in as a group.

"Most of the people like us that you might run across, however, never find a group like this. They end up spending most of their lives alone. Of course, it's better to be alone and be yourself than to not be alone and forget who you are, which is what I think most people end up doing."

Kate looked over at the house as she listened to John and tried to process what he said. "You really amaze me, John. I think the problem is that you never act like you're as smart as you are. I mean, most people who are really smart are rather arrogant about it. You're a living contradiction, and the proof of that is on the shelves in your living room. You're the only person I know who listens to Mozart and Meatloaf, and I always thought that the people who read Shakespeare were balding, old English professors. Everything you do is done with confidence and foresight, yet you don't have the courage to ask out the one girl you really like. You can't even accept the idea that she really wants you to."

"I'm not really all that smart, Kate. It's just that guys like me generally have a lot of time on their hands for things like thinking and reading. As far as Chris is concerned, hammers and paint brushes are one thing—I can handle those, but I've never been all that good at dealing with people."

"I'd say that you're a whole lot better at dealing with people than you give yourself credit for, and a heck of a lot smarter as well. If you were a Christian, I bet you'd make one heck of an evangelist."

"And I suppose that if I was a Christian, I'd automatically have all this confidence you say I need?"

"No, not really, but God's strength could help you get around it. There's something I wanted to talk to you about. You know that I've been talking a lot with Chris, and I think that she's just about ready to ask God to come into her life."

"Yeah, I know that. Actually, I think she's been just about ready for a long time. She's just never had anyone around to answer her questions before the way you have. That's one of the reason's I'm glad you've been around the past couple of days. She's needed someone to answer her questions that the rest of us don't have the answers to."

Kate sat down on the ground and began playing with a stick. "I think there's more holding her back than just her questions. I think the one thing that's really holding her up is that she doesn't know how you'd react to it. She's already more than half-convinced that you don't want her around, and I think she's afraid that a change like that would drive you away for real. You, and what you think, are very important to her. She's not going to do anything if she thinks she'll lose you doing it. I'm glad you don't mind me talking to her, and that you're even happy for her. It makes it a lot easier to ask you to do me a favor."

John also sat down on the ground and leaned back until he was resting on his elbows. "I'd be happy to do anything I can for you."

"Well, this is a little more than just picking something up at the store for me. I really believe that coming to know Jesus would be the best thing that ever happened to Chris, but that will never happen unless she knows that you're going to support her, whatever decision she makes. Chris is going to church with me in the morning, and I thought that if you were there to support her, it might give her the strength to go ahead and do it. I don't know what your feelings about church are, but I'm asking you to do this for Chris, and for me."

"You know, you have it almost right, but not completely. I don't think that what's holding Chris back is me, exactly, because she knows that I'm going to be there for her no matter what. Remember what I told you about 'other people,' well that's Chris all the way. What Chris fears more than anything else is being alone. That's the one thing that will make all of us do just about anything. We've all been alone, and none of us ever want to be there again. We'll do anything to avoid losing these few friends, or in this case, leave them behind. What's going to be important for Chris is that there is a friend waiting for her on the other side, and it doesn't have to be me. That's what is going to make the difference in her making this decision."

"So you're not going to go." It wasn't a question.

"The last time I went to a church was the day they buried my mom. Since then, I haven't been able to even look at a church without seeing that scared, lonely little boy, crying in the corner while everyone ignored him. Everything even remotely connected to church brings up things I would just as soon not remember. I prefer to remember my mom the way she was when she was alive. Things like her eyes that laughed and cried at the same time. Like how she always seemed to know where I was and when I needed a hug or a swat. No, I don't really want to go, but I will. I can't promise that I'm going to be able to sit through the service or anything. But I'll try because, if this is going to make Chris happy, then I want to be there to see it. Maybe it's a little selfish, but I want to be a part of that."

"Thanks, John. Like I said, sometimes you amaze me. Who knows, maybe you'll get something out of it too."

"I guess that's possible, but I wouldn't get my hopes up if I were you. I made my peace with God when my mother died. The two of us haven't had much to say to each other since then. Are you going to bull whip Brad into going?"

"Already taken care of. It didn't take a lot of convincing on my part, though. I guess he really does want to spend time with me, wherever that might be. I'm not going to argue with him about it either. Being with him just feels right. It's the second best feeling in the world."

"Just remember, Brad is like a brother to me. If you take Brad, you get the rest of us in a package deal, and that's just the way I like it."

"Don't worry, I'm not going to take him away. In fact, I sort of like hanging around with you guys, so if you'll have me, I'm thinking I'd like to stick around myself."

"It's too late for that; you're already in. Just remember that what you have here is a lot more than just friends."

"Well, isn't that the way it's supposed to be? I'm going to find Brad; maybe you should go find Chris."

"That sounds like a good idea. I bet that fire is just about ready to cook on. It's been so long since I've had something to eat that my stomach is beginning to think my throat's been cut."

※

The cook-out was not exactly five-star fare, but then there's definitely a place in this world for grilled burgers and corn on the cob. Throw in a few brats, and there was plenty to satisfy everyone, even Ricky. After polishing off his fourth burger, Ricky leaned back against a tree. "You know, if we could just figure out a way to grill fries, I'd never have to leave this spot. There's nothing like good food, and plenty of it, to make a man feel satisfied." Ricky looked over at Shannon and winked at her. "Well, almost nothing anyway."

Chris threw a stick at him, which missed by quite a bit. "Before he starts rhapsodizing about all the things that make him happy, what do you say we turn on some tunes? What we need right now is some good music."

John got up and walked over to the tape player, which was set back away from the fire. "That can be arranged. Anybody got any special requests?"

"How about some REO," April called out. "Before you guys start playing your heavy metal, I'd like to hear some feel-good music."

"REO I can do, but you'll have to settle for some of their older stuff. How about the live album?"

"That's fine," April said. "I just have to work my way up to Rush and Ratt, if you know what I mean." John turned on the tape player, loud enough to be heard but quiet enough that it wouldn't interfere with the conversation, and walked back to sit near the fire. "I don't see how anyone would have to work their way up to Rush. After all, we're talking about one of the finest bands in the world."

"I can see that," Lee said, "but their lyrics get a little deep for me. I prefer songs I can understand."

"I take it then that the two of you won't be going to the concert next week."

Lee gave a slight shrug. "No, I have to work anyway. Some of us don't have regular jobs and have to work weekends."

"I've told you before, if you want a job at the print shop, there's plenty of room. I know there are at least three openings right now. Just say the word, and I'll get you in."

"I don't think so. The smell of all that ink makes me dizzy. Plus, I'm going to be leaving for boot camp in three weeks."

For several days, John's focus had been primarily Chris, and he hadn't really paid much attention to what was going on with his other friends. He looked around at them now, and was somewhat startled by what he saw. Ricky was sitting against another tree with Shannon sitting between his legs resting her head on his shoulder. Lee and April weren't touching, but they were sitting closer together than they had in a while. Across from them, Brad and Kate were sitting next to each other, holding hands and stealing glances at each other. Only he and Chris were sitting by themselves. "I need to check on something," John said as he stood. "I'll be right back."

John walked around to the front of the house and sat down on the stairs. He was just sitting there, staring out at the road when Ricky came up to join him. "What's up, dude? You're acting kind of weird tonight."

"What do you mean, weird?"

"I mean it's not like you to just get up and walk off like that. Then I come out here and find you sitting by yourself."

"I don't know, Ricky. I've never minded sitting by myself before. Mostly, I think, because we were all sitting by ourselves, except for Lee and April, and even they spent more time sitting across from each other than next to each other. Now, you're over sitting with Shannon, Brad's sitting beside Kate, and even Lee and April are sitting together—and I'm still sitting by myself. It's funny, I always thought that you were the only thing that might come between Chris and me, but now you're out of the picture, and it's Rich that's coming between us.

"Don't get me wrong, I think it's great that you and Shannon got hooked up, and it's about time Brad started acting like a mortal. It's just that there seems to be even more dead air between Chris and me than ever, and now it seems that the rest of you are leaving me behind as well. It just sort of hit me all at once, and I had to get away for a bit, that's all."

Ricky sat down next to John and stared out at the road. "John, I'm the last person in the world who should be giving anybody advice on girls, but I think that you're making this a lot more complicated than it should be. Maybe you should stop listening to what Chris says with her mouth and start paying attention to what the rest of her is saying. You've probably never noticed the way she looks at you when you're looking the other way, but you can't tell me that you don't see how she looks at you when you're looking right at each other. Even when she's on the opposite side of the room, she's always leaning toward you. Haven't you noticed that you're the only guy Chris has touched all week? She's starting to talk to the rest of us, but there's almost always something between us when she does. If not, there's plenty of room to give her a head start toward the door. She's not quite ready to trust me and Brad and Lee, but she's never stopped trusting you. The way I see it, the only thing coming between you and Chris is you. Until you stop making excuses, you're going to continue to be sitting by yourself."

"Let's just say you're right, and I go out there and sit down next to Chris. What am I supposed to do if she freaks out? If she gets up and, like, moves away from me, I just might lose it."

"John, you ain't never 'lost it,' and you're not going to start tonight, no matter what happens. But you are going to be sitting out here, beating yourself up over this until you do something about it. Things are going to get harder the longer you wait. Besides, how long do you think she's going to wait for you? Look, she wants to be with you as much as you want to be with her, and right now, she needs you, even if she can't admit it."

"I guess you're right. Besides, that road isn't going to do anything exciting anytime soon. Let's get back to the fire."

John and Ricky walked back to where the others were. When they got there, Kate was changing the tape, and the rest were still sitting in the same places they were when John left. Ricky gave John a good-natured punch in the shoulder and went back to his place between Shannon and the tree. John walked over and sat just a couple of inches from Chris and silently reached out to place his hand on top of hers. As Kate went back to her place beside Brad, Chris turned her head to look at John. There was fear and confusion in her expression. John also thought he saw a trace of hope and something else that he hoped was a positive sign.

Chris did move her hand away from John's, but only so that she could move closer to him. She then grabbed his hand with both of hers and hesitantly laid her head on his shoulders. For the first time in as long as he could remember, everything in John's world seemed right. He failed to notice the smiles on his friends' faces.

Chapter 12

When John woke up the next morning, he couldn't remember a night that he had ever slept so well. He had not been aware of the tension that had been building up in him, and finally making things right with Chris had relieved much of it. Last night seemed like a bridge between then and now. This morning was so much different from any day before that he was certain that this was a new beginning. Even the idea that he had promised to go to church with Chris and Kate didn't really seem like a mistake like it had yesterday.

That would have to work itself out. John walked over to the window to look out on what sort of day was coming. The sky was cloudy, and it definitely looked like it was going to rain. He could even smell it coming, something that John had only realized was possible after he had been living out here for a while. As a rule, John didn't really like rain, but today, it somehow seemed appropriate, as though it was ready to wash away the past.

Down and across the hall, Chris was also getting out of bed. Last night had been the best night of her life, but she somehow sensed that it was not a new beginning. It was just a step toward bringing that new beginning to life. Chris felt that there was something else she needed to really make that change, and she desperately hoped that she would find it this morning at Kate's church. It wasn't that last night had been any less important for her.

John had kissed her for the first time last night as they were saying good night. She had dreamed of that moment for a long time, and when it came, it was even better than she dreamt of. The one thing that she hadn't expected from that moment was to wake up the next morning alone in her own bed. She couldn't ever remember when someone had kissed her without expectations for what came after. Chris could almost see God working all this out. Maybe God wasn't as disappointed in her as she had always thought he would be.

❦

For Kate, the coming day held a great deal of hope, but it also promised a great deal of anxiety. With the questions about her relationship with Brad out of the way for now, leading her new friends to Christ was the most important thing in her life. As close as Chris was, Kate knew that it would take just a small nudge in the right direction. She also knew that a single misstep could ruin everything.

Kate sat on the edge of her bed and closed her eyes in prayer to ask God for direction, guidance, and grace. As she prayed, she touched her hand to the necklace Brad had given her, and thanked God for bringing him into her life. Afterward, Kate turned on her radio and hummed along to the music as she went about getting ready. Chris could never imagine that today was just as important to Kate as it was for her, only in a much different way.

❦

John walked out of his room and headed for the stairs. As he passed Chris's room, he could hear her moving around and decided to knock on her door instead. When she answered the door, Chris was wearing a robe and was in the process of fixing her hair, something she hadn't done all week. John leaned over and kissed her on the cheek. "Good morning, gorgeous. I just thought I'd stop by and see if you were ready to dump me yet."

"Not hardly. I tried to warn you, but you wouldn't listen. You're stuck with me now." Chris opened the door all the way and moved back to make room. "Come on in. You can keep me company while I fix my hair. Since I haven't done anything with it all week, it's a total mess. It's going to take me all morning to make it look good enough to be seen in public."

John walked in and sat on the edge of the bed, while Chris attacked her hair with a curling iron. "If you want my opinion, it looked fine the way it was."

"I think that opinion might just be a little biased, John. I look like one of the orphans from *Oliver Twist*."

"I suppose that my opinion might be a little prejudiced, but isn't that the way it's supposed to work? Even if it is, though, that doesn't mean that it's wrong. So, how did you sleep last night?"

"Last night was the best night's sleep I've had all week. It wasn't great, but then that bed isn't really all that great either."

"What do you expect? This bed's been around a long time. I suppose that we'll have to see about getting you a new bed if you plan on sticking around for a while."

"Is that your not-so-subtle way of asking me to move in here for good?"

"Something like that. I want to spend as much time with you as I can. It's not like you have anyplace else to go, and this is just as much your home as it is mine. I want you to stay, but only if you're comfortable with it."

Chris put the curling iron down and walked over to sit on the bed next to John. "I've really been hoping you'd ask me to stay, but before I say yes, we need to talk about us first. I want to be with you more than anything else in the world, John, but I need you to understand that I can't sleep with you. At least, I can't right now."

John reached over to hold her hand. "I know that, Chris. It's going to take you some time to get over what happened the other day. Also, if things work out today the way I think they're going to, it'll probably be even longer. When you're ready, you'll let me know. It's not exactly what I had in mind, but that's the reality we have. Now that I've got you, I'm not going to do anything to risk losing you."

"It's not exactly the way I thought it would be, either. It's hard for me to imagine what a relationship would be like without sex, but I think I'd like to try it. Who knows; maybe it'll make things better for us. You're right, someday I will be ready, and when that day comes, I know it'll be wonderful."

"Well, for right now, I guess I'll have to settle for a kiss, and then I'll go and make us a pot of coffee." John kissed her and then stood and walked toward the door. "Would you do me a favor, though? Don't get too carried away with your hair. I really do like it better when it's not quite so made up."

Chris smiled at him as she walked back over to the mirror. "I promise, I'll keep it simple, but I've got to do something with it. This is going to be my first time in church, and I want to look my best."

"You've never looked otherwise. I'll see you downstairs."

John closed the door behind him and went down to the kitchen. He was surprised to find that Brad was also up and had beaten him to the coffeepot. The coffee was already brewing when he walked in, and Brad was sitting at the table eating a bowl of cereal. "You're up early. I figured we were going to have to come up and drag you out of bed like we usually do."

"Actually, I've been up for almost an hour. Believe it or not, I've been awake most of the night thinking about church. I just couldn't get past the idea that something big was going to happen today. I never thought that the idea of going to church would affect me like this."

John poured himself a glass of milk and sat down to wait for the coffee to finish brewing. "Are you sure that it's church that's doing it, or could it be the thought of seeing Kate again?"

Brad polished off his cereal and wiped the corners of his mouth with his fingers. "No, I don't think that it's just the idea of seeing Kate again. There's more to it than that. I mean, I really didn't sleep very well the night before either because I was thinking about giving her that necklace all night. This was different, though. I just couldn't shake the feeling that this was going to be a big day. I can't explain it any better than that. You'll just have to take my word for it."

"Actually, I think I know what you mean. I had the same kind of feeling, but mostly I had a lot of other things to think about."

"Yeah, well it's about time you took care of that little bit of business. The two of you were beginning to make me a little nauseous. I never thought I'd have a girlfriend before you did."

"Yeah, well that's the kind of week it's been." John got up and poured himself and Brad a cup of coffee and then carried both cups back to the table and sat down. "Actually, I probably would never have gone through with it if it wasn't for the fact that both you and Ricky had girlfriends. I guess you could say I was feeling sort of left out."

"Speaking of Ricky, did you know that he and Shannon didn't come back last night? They were just coming in when I was getting up this morning. He said that they were downtown and spent the entire night at Memorial Park. I never would have thought those two would get together."

"Whatever works for them, dude. I think that he might be considering giving up on the idea of going to Colorado. It would get awfully boring around here without him to get into trouble with every so often."

"Like we can't do enough of that on our own? Not to change the subject, but I'm going to anyway. How do you want to handle this today? Do you think we should all ride over to Kate's house together, or do you just want to follow me over there?"

"We probably ought to take two cars, because there's no telling what's going to happen afterward. For all I know, the girls might well decide to go off and leave us for whatever reason. Those two are getting to be pretty close. You know, except for dinner that one night and a quick run to the shop, this will be the first time I've gotten out of here since the party. I don't know what anyone else has planned, but I might want to do something afterward myself, even if it's just to grab some lunch somewhere."

"Well, Ricky and Shannon will be sleeping all day, but do you think we could get Lee and April to join us?"

"You might be able to talk April into going, but there is no way you'd be able to talk Lee into it. I'm not sure what it is that he has against church, but I know that it's all he can do to tolerate Kate. I don't think we could trust him to keep his cool if we did get him to go."

"Yeah, that's true. It was just a thought. I guess it'll be the four of us."

❦

Kate was in the kitchen helping her mother get things ready for Sunday dinner. She put the lid on the salad bowl and placed it in the refrigerator. "Are you sure you don't mind doing this, Mom?"

"Of course I don't mind. I've always told you that you're welcome to have your friends over for Sunday dinner. Besides, I'm looking forward to meeting them."

"I know, but there are as many of them as there are of us. There may even be more than just the three, but I sort of doubt it."

"There's plenty here if any more show up. It doesn't really change anything, at least until you get to the part where you have to clean it all up."

"Well, thank you for doing this anyway. The three that I know are coming have never really had much of a family life. I want them to see that things can be better."

"You've been telling me about Brad for nine months now, and you've talked a lot about Chris the past few days, but you haven't really said much about this other guy, John. What's his story?"

"John is Brad's best friend and Chris's boyfriend. I'm not real sure what to make of John. He just may be the smartest person I've ever met, and he seems to be a really great guy. To hear the others talk about him, you'd think he was some sort of saint or something. I haven't really had the chance to get to know him all that well, but I get the impression that the only thing he's missing in his life is Jesus. I don't know; it almost seems like he's too perfect, if you know what I mean."

Kate's mother put the roast in the oven and set the timer so it would cook while they were at church. "Maybe he is. You know, there are a lot of really good people out there who are not saved that live better lives than some of the people who claim to be Christians. Only God and time can say for sure."

"You know, I was talking with him a little last night, and he said something that really rang true for me. He was telling me some about who he was, and I haven't been able to stop thinking about it since. I think it might be very important."

"And just what did he say about himself?"

"He was talking about how people tend to gather in groups, and he said that anyone outside that group would be referred to as 'other people.' Anyway, he was saying that he and the rest of them were never able to fit into any of those cliques and so they're 'other people.' He said they were all people who never really belonged anywhere until they got together with each other. John also said that there were others like him out there who were never able to find a group of friends like he has, and they either end up living their lives alone or compromise who they are just to fit in."

"Like you said, John sounds like a smart guy. He's right. There are a lot of people out there who never seem to fit in and end up alone, and there are many who seem to go along just so they can fit in. What people like that need is to have God in their hearts, but I'd bet John didn't figure that into his theory, did he?"

"No, he didn't. The point is that it seemed as though he was trying to tell me something, but he didn't know how to say it. Do you think I was imagining things?"

"Maybe he's scared that he's going to end up alone. It's possible that he was trying to ask if you knew a way to make sure that wouldn't happen. There's nothing more frightening than the thought of being all alone in the world."

"I think I might have missed an opportunity."

"Don't worry about it too much. If he really is looking for something, then I'm sure he'll give you another chance. Keep in mind that people don't always say what they mean, Kate, especially when they are not sure themselves what they mean."

"It's just that John can be sort of intimidating to talk to. You just know that he could make a fool out of you if he really wanted to, and I get the impression that he just might do that every so often, just for fun. I don't know that I'm prepared to deal with John. That's why I was so happy to get him to agree to go to church this morning. I think that maybe Pastor Henry could get through to him where I couldn't."

Mrs. Knight was about to say something when the doorbell rang. "That's probably them. Why don't you go let your friends in, and we'll just see what happens."

Kate walked into the living room only to find that her father had already opened the door, and Brad, Chris, and John were coming through. Kate was impressed with the way they looked. Brad was wearing slacks and a tie and, in Kate's opinion, looking very handsome. John was wearing black jeans and a dress shirt. He almost looked like a young Johnny Cash. It was Chris, though, who really stood out. Chris had done such a good job of hiding the way she looked since Kate had met her that Kate almost didn't recognize her. Her strawberry-blonde hair hung in loose curls over her shoulders, and she was wearing a flattering, though very modest, dress. They almost looked like three different people. "When you said you'd be here at ten, you weren't joking."

Chris wrapped her arms nervously around John's and pulled him closer to her. "We practically had to put a leash on Brad. If he had his way, we'd have been here two hours ago."

"That would've been all right. Come on in and sit down. We're not quite ready to leave yet. We normally go to Sunday school, but since you guys were coming, we thought that we'd just do the worship service this morning. I hope that you don't have any plans for after church."

"Not really," Brad said. "What did you have in mind?"

As they all took seats in the living room, Mr. Knight said, "We thought that you might enjoy having Sunday dinner with us this afternoon. It's one of our little Sunday rituals."

Sitting next to Chris on the couch, John said, "When it comes to food, you only have to ask me once, though it's probably a good thing that Ricky didn't come after all. I doubt that there's that much food in this house."

Kate smiled and said, "You might be right there. I'm sorry, I haven't introduced you yet. Dad, this is John and Chris, and of course you've already met Brad."

John let go of Chris's hand only long enough to stand and reach out to shake Mr. Knight's hand. "How are you doing, sir? It's good to meet you."

Mr. Knight returned his firm handshake. "It's always good to meet Kate's friends. She's told us a lot about you."

As he returned to his seat, John smiled and winked at Kate. "Do I at least get to present my side of the story?"

Mr. Knight chuckled. "I'll be sure to give you that chance. For now, though, just relax for a moment, and we'll be ready as soon as Caroline is finished in the kitchen. Actually, I think I should go and see if she needs any help."

Mr. Knight walked off toward the kitchen, leaving the four of them alone. Kate sat down next to Brad on the loveseat. "Are you guys sure that you don't mind eating here? I don't want to make you feel uncomfortable or anything."

"Are you kidding?" Brad asked as he put his arm around Kate. "I haven't had a really good home-cooked meal in years. Lee does a decent job with the grill, and John here makes a mean cup of coffee, but those aren't the same."

Chris had relaxed some after Mr. Knight left the room, but she still seemed very tense. "I don't know if John even knows how to turn the oven on. Then again, neither do I."

"Just laugh it up you two. Next time, I'll let Ricky do the cooking."

"Are you saying that Ricky can't cook either?" Kate asked.

"We have no idea," Brad answered. "There's never enough left over for anyone to find out."

"You guys are horrible. He isn't even here to defend himself."

Mr. and Mrs. Knight walked into the room and announced that they were ready to leave. They decided to take two cars and leave Chris's parked out front.

Everyone got in a car, and Brad followed Mr. Knight to the Long Ridge Church of Grace.

Sunday school classes were just getting out when the six of them entered the church. It wasn't a small building, but it wasn't really very large either. The pale, off-white walls were contrasted by the rich brown oak that seemed to be everywhere. The only real decoration in the room was the large cross behind the altar.

Mr. and Mrs. Knight took their accustomed places toward the front of the center section, while Kate, Brad, John, and Chris found seats toward the middle of the right-hand section. As people began to fill in the pews around them, several stopped to say hello and shake hands with the three visitors.

After shaking hand with an elderly gentleman, John sat back down next to Chris and leaned over to whisper in her ear, "This is a lot different than the last time I was in one of these places. The last time I was in church, I don't think anyone even noticed I was there."

Although Chris had been very nervous before they got there, she now felt much more relaxed, and she was beginning to notice how tightly John was holding her hand. "If you really feel uncomfortable, John, I'll understand if you need to leave."

"This isn't about me, it's about you. This just might be a big day for you, and I don't want to miss it. I'm a big boy now; I think I can handle a little bit of discomfort."

Chris didn't say anything. She simply smiled at him, glad that he wanted to be here for her.

Soon, the service began, and everyone stood and began singing. Some of the songs were ones that Chris recognized from the services she had seen on TV, others were completely new to her, but she thought they all sounded beautiful. There was a short break in the singing to open the service in prayer, and then everyone began singing again.

After the music had finished playing and everyone had taken their seats again, a man stepped forward to recognize the visitors in the congregation. Kate stood to introduce her guests as her boyfriend and two of her very best friends, after which even more people gathered around to welcome them.

Chris was very nearly overwhelmed by the sheer number of people who all seemed sincerely happy to meet her. Deep inside, a warmth surrounded her heart and began to move outward to envelop her entire body. She never thought that she could feel so comfortable and so welcome among this many strangers. She squeezed John's hand excitedly, and when Chris looked at him, there was a strange expression on his face.

After the introductions, another man stepped up to the podium to ask for prayer requests. Kate raised her hand for an unspoken request, though Chris thought that she might know what it was about. When all the requests were taken, the entire church began to pray, out loud, and all at the same time, but not together. She tried to hear what was being said at the altar, but the prayers of those around her made it difficult to make out. At last, she gave up, drew her thoughts to herself, and began to really pray for the first time in her life.

Ricky was dead tired, but he couldn't sleep. He and Shannon had been out all night, walking through the streets of downtown. They had started out at Memorial Park, just walking around holding hands like all the other couples that gathered there on Saturday nights. It wasn't long, though, before they left the park to wander the city streets. They spent the entire night walking around talking, and they just never seemed to run out of things to say to each other. Before they knew it, the sun was beginning to stain the eastern sky with its dusty red light.

They got back to the house just as Brad was getting up, and they went immediately upstairs before anyone else started stirring. Ricky had some ideas about what he wanted to do once they got there, and sleep wasn't one of them. It seemed as though Shannon had the same ideas because she had walked right into his bedroom with him.

Sleep, however, had been too hard to resist, and she was soon passed out on Ricky's bed. Rather than fight it, Ricky also fell asleep, but he didn't sleep for long. He woke up just in time to hear Brad's van pull out of the driveway. Even though his body cried out for sleep, his mind was wide awake. He got up from the bed and went over to a chair in the corner where he could watch Shannon as she slept.

A week ago, he would never have given a second thought to giving up on his plans to leave for Colorado and not come back, but that was before he met Shannon. What really amazed Ricky though, was the fact that a couple of girls had managed to drag both John and Brad to church. Ricky wanted no part of church, but he couldn't get over the feeling that he was somehow missing something.

Chris and John were the two best friends he had—maybe the only real friends. Sure, he had Shannon in his life now, but there was no way she could take the place of the two people who had given him so much. Now, they were off looking for a new life. They weren't really going anywhere, but regardless of what happened this morning, there were bound to be changes, and Ricky had enough of change to last him for quite some time. Maybe there was more to this church thing than he realized. Then again, maybe not.

April was not at all happy with the way things were going. To begin with, she was alone, and that was not a situation that she liked at all. Ricky and Shannon had just gone to bed, and Lee still wasn't out of his. The others had all gone off to church, and who knew when they would get back. The TV didn't really work all that well, and there was nothing on the radio worth listening to on Sunday mornings. All that left April alone with her thoughts, and thinking was not something she really liked to do. It wasn't that she was stupid or lazy; it was more that she just wasn't all that comfortable with herself. April sat alone at the kitchen table, drinking coffee and thinking—and she wasn't very impressed by what she was learning about herself.

What April was beginning to understand was that she had never *had* to be alone. She always had friends—though she was happier with the current ones—and she had always seemed to have a boyfriend. The idea that now rocked her world was that she didn't really want a boyfriend, at least not the one she had. In a moment of complete self-honesty, April admitted to herself that she really didn't even like Lee all that much. There was just a certain amount of comfort in the thought of having a relationship, and as long as Lee was around, she wasn't alone.

April finished her coffee and set the cup down on the table. "This is crazy," she told the cup. "I'm sitting around analyzing myself and talking to a coffee cup."

She got up from the table and went outside to find something to do. Without thinking much about what she was doing, she found herself out on the road walking toward where it ended. About a half mile down from the gate, the road came to an old bridge where it crossed a stream. The road didn't really end on the other side, but it was blocked by a huge gate. A sign on the gate proclaimed that it was government property and to stay out. April didn't care about going farther anyway. She stopped in the middle of the bridge and looked down on the water rushing past on its way to the river.

Despite herself, April was still lost in her thoughts. There were no earth-shattering realizations, but she did learn a lot about herself in just a few minutes. Hoping that Lee might be up, she turned and walked back to the house.

⚇

There was one more song after the prayer requests. Brad liked to sing, but he didn't know the words and felt of out of place just standing there. He looked over to where John and Chris were standing and noticed that they were both in about the same situation he was. Then came the offering, which really made Brad uncomfortable. As he passed the plate to Kate, he watched as she dropped a couple of bills in, and then she turned and smiled at him as she passed it on.

Once the collection had been taken, the pastor got up to the podium to speak. Up to this point, Brad had been easily distracted by all that was going on around him, but this was what the whole morning was supposed to be about, so he settled into his seat and focused his attention on the man at the front of the church.

Pastor Henry started behind the podium, but he didn't stay there for long. Brad had prepared himself for a classroom-type lecture and was taken off guard by Pastor Henry. As he talked, the pastor was animated, he was passionate, and he was clearly excited by his subject. Brad quickly got over his initial shock and soon found himself scarcely breathing as he listened to Pastor Henry and his message.

Large parts of the sermon were beyond Brad, things that were clearly meant for those who were long-time churchgoers, but mostly it was about the simplicity of God's grace. It was this very simplicity that appealed to Brad. He had spent most of his life trying to simplify things so he could understand life, and although he was still trying, he was no closer to realizing his goal than he had been when he was ten. This, though, he could understand.

Shannon had never been a sound sleeper. The slightest sound during the night was often enough to wake her. During the day, she slept even lighter. When Ricky got out of the bed, she woke up, a little confused. What was she doing in bed with Ricky? After a moment, she realized that they were both still dressed, and then she remembered how she ended up there. Shannon lay there quietly and watched him as he moved around the room. When he sat down in the chair, she relaxed and went back to sleep.

When Shannon woke up some time later, she could sense that Ricky was still sitting in the chair, watching her sleep. She opened her eyes and rolled over to look at him. "Why aren't you sleeping?"

"I tried, but it didn't work."

"Well, try again. I can't sleep with you staring at me."

Ricky didn't say anything. He just got back in the bed and lay down next to her. Soon he was asleep, and it was Shannon's turn to not be able to sleep. Shannon lay there watching his back as he snored softly. She found it difficult to believe the situation she was in. When she finally admitted to herself what was happening between her and Ricky, she swore that it would be a long time before she slept with him, yet here she was, lying in his bed. True, nothing had happened, but that was only because they were both too tired by the time they got back this morning. When she followed him into the room and sat on the edge of his bed this morning, it was with the intention of having sex with him.

Now, she didn't know what to do. Shannon was no virgin, but her relationship with Isaac had been all about sex, and she didn't want the same thing to happen between her and Ricky. She wanted Ricky to love her regardless of the sex. At the same time though, she wanted more than anything to be with him, to feel him next to her, and to hold him tight and not let go. She knew they had to talk about it, but she was afraid of how he might respond. This relationship had to be about more than just sex, but Shannon didn't want to lose him because of it either.

If she had consciously chased after Ricky, it would have been a lot easier, but hooking up with him hadn't really crossed her mind until it happened. They found each other by accident, or maybe it was fate, but either way it seemed to have the makings of something really special. She didn't want to do anything that might ruin it. Maybe this evening she could corner Chris and get her opinion. Ricky was close to Chris, and if there was anyone who could guess what he would say, it would be her.

Another problem that she was going to have to face was telling her parents. She figured that they would flip out over the whole thing. They both seemed to like Ricky, but both she and Ricky had assured her parents that there was nothing going on between them. Now, they had made all that a lie. It was possible that they would understand what had brought her and Ricky together, but the idea that she was staying out here with him was bound to do bad things for their sense of humor. Shannon was trying to come up with a good way to explain everything, when she quietly slipped back to sleep.

———

Before Pastor Henry had said more than five sentences, John knew why he had come. Unlike Brad and Chris, he was not completely enthralled with the message, but he could see a definite purpose for him being here. He could tell by the way that Chris was holding his hand that she was thoroughly wrapped up in the sermon, and one look at Brad showed quite plainly that he too was caught up. John picked up a Bible that had been sitting on the pew and dutifully looked up whichever passage the pastor was referring to.

For John, the message was very clear. We can't get to heaven on our own. It is only by the grace of God and his unconditional love that we are saved. John had never really stopped believing in God, but he had always held on to the hope that he could work his way into heaven. He was a good person, though maybe a little rough around the edges, and he always thought that might be enough to get him through. Now, he was beginning to see that it wasn't enough. If there was any way he was going to see heaven, it was going to take a commitment on his part, a commitment to love God. That was what it was all about: making a commitment.

———

Kate could scarcely believe what was happening. She had been pretty sure that Chris was about ready to make her decision, but had not dared to hope for getting through to either Brad or John for some time to come. What she was seeing now, though, reaffirmed her faith in the power of God. It was plain that Brad was now ready to make his own decision, and it seemed that John was on the verge. There was no doubt that the hand of God was moving here. Kate bowed her head and said a quick prayer of thanks and then looked back at her friends. John looked back at her, so she smiled at him and returned her attention to Pastor Henry.

Pastor Henry concluded the sermon with an altar call. He asked everyone to bow their heads and pray that those being called would respond. Chris had never felt so strongly about anything in her life. Nearly from the moment that the pastor began speaking, she felt herself filled with wonder and joy. There was no way she could hold back any longer.

Even before everyone had bowed their heads, Chris was moving. She had said the prayer, asking Jesus to come into her life, and he did. Chris now knew what Kate had meant about feeling the hand of God. She could almost hear him speaking to her; welcoming her home and telling her how much he loved her. She could almost see the angels as they rejoiced at another soul saved. There was nothing "almost" about the feel of God's touch.

Chris could feel the weight being lifted from her shoulders and the presence of a steady hand offering support. Last night, Chris had been sure that nothing could ever feel as good as John's arm wrapped around her shoulders, but that was nothing compared to the feel of the arms that were holding her now; arms that she knew would never let her go.

When she reached the altar, Chris knelt down with tears of joy streaming from her eyes and thanked God for coming into her life. She was only vaguely aware of the woman who came to kneel beside her until she placed her hand on Chris's shoulder and began to ask her some questions. Chris answered the questions but focused most of her attention on the feeling she had inside her heart.

After some time, the woman pulled Chris off to the side and began to read various passages from the Bible to her. She then gave Chris a small Bible, said it was a gift from the church, and encouraged her to read it often. Chris held it tightly to her chest and wept even harder. She had never felt so loved in her life. When at last she looked up, she was surprised to see both John and Brad also kneeling at the altar.

⌘

Brad was wavering when the pastor first gave the altar call. The things he heard made sense. The answer was simple, but there was something missing. Although everyone was supposed to have their heads bowed, Brad looked around some after he made room for Chris to get out. He watched as she knelt at the altar. For the first time since he had met her, Chris looked truly happy. Even though she was crying uncontrollably, there was something about the way she held her head and the set of her shoulders that plainly said there was no sorrow in those tears. It was at that point that something broke inside Brad's heart.

Brad had always made it a point to make sure that he kept his emotions under tight control, but he couldn't keep them in check any longer. Years of pent-up emotions burst out, and Brad knew that he would never be the same again. All the pain, sorrow, fear, and loneliness that he had kept locked up deep inside broke loose. The wave of emotions sweeping over him nearly knocked him off his feet, literally. Brad found that he had to hold on to the back of the pew in front of him just to keep standing, but he didn't stand there for long. He felt Kate's questioning hand on his arm, and in an instant he made his decision and he was moving.

Brad had not said the prayer of invitation along with the pastor, but as he knelt at the altar, the words poured from both his mouth and his heart. He prayed with a passion he never knew he had, felt things he never knew he could feel, and said things he never thought he'd say. For just a moment, he lost himself in the moment until the touch of a hand on his shoulder brought him back to reality.

The man who had come to kneel next to him gently guided him through the prayer of invitation once again and then led him to a pew where he began to ask Brad some questions. Brad was also given a Bible, which he immediately opened and began to flip through the pages until he came to one that seemed to capture his attention and sum up everything that was happening. First John 4:18 (NIV) said, "There is no fear in love. But perfect love drives out fear." It was all so simple, why had it taken him so long to see it? Brad looked up to see John being led away from the altar. With all that he was going through, he wasn't surprised to see tears running down John's face.

The thing about commitments was that they work in two directions. John had never had a problem committing himself to anything, but he had always shied away from expecting anyone to commit themselves to him. He never expected anything from anyone, but he desperately wanted to feel whatever it was that he could see in Chris and Brad. The problem was that something held him back.

John kept his eyes on Chris as she knelt at the altar. She deserved this, and he didn't want to miss any part of what she was experiencing. He felt a certain amount of peace in knowing that she had found something to make her happy. He was so intent on watching Chris that he nearly jumped when Kate laid her hand on his and said, "You know, John, God won't ever abandon you. He doesn't want you to ever be alone again, and you don't need to compromise who you are to have what he offers. God loves you for who you are, and he always will." That was all she said, and then she went back to watching the drama unfolding at the front of the church.

At first, John didn't understand why Kate would say that. He started to say something to her; to tell her that she didn't know what she was talking about, when he felt his eyes start to water. He hadn't cried since his mother's funeral, and he tried to fight it back now, but couldn't. He sat down in the pew and began to cry like a baby. Through the tears, he cried out to God, "Please, God, tell me if it's true. Could even you love me? Is your love really so great that you could love a worthless man like me? I really need to know."

John never honestly expected God to answer, so it took a while for him to realize what was happening. He didn't so much hear the answer as feel it.

When he finally understood that the warm feeling coming over him was the answer he was looking for, John jumped over the ledge into God's embrace. He would never be able to remember making his way to the altar. The only memory to stay with him was the single thought that raced constantly around in his mind: God loved him.

He knew that this was the place he was supposed to be as he knelt at the altar, but he had no idea what to do next. When Pastor Henry knelt down beside him, John pleaded with him for help. "I want Jesus in my life, but I don't know how to ask." So the pastor guided him through the prayer and then led him over to the pew next to where Chris was sitting. He asked some questions, which John answered, and gave him a Bible. John had a couple of Bibles at home, and had even read through them a few times, but this small, inexpensive gift meant more to him than anything he owned.

John leaned back in the pew to try to take in everything that had happened. He had difficulty understanding that it had all taken place. He looked over at Chris and smiled at her when she looked back. He reached out his hand to hold hers and was grateful for the comfort of her touch. John could not believe how exhausted he was.

Kate did not know why she said the things she did to John, but she suspected that it was really the Spirit talking through her. Somehow, the words he needed to hear were right there in her head. She hadn't dared to hope that all three of her friends would come to accept Jesus today. Kate had, of course, thought about it and prayed for it, but she had accepted that it was going to take some more time for Brad and John. God had revealed to her his awesome power, though, and she was slightly ashamed of herself for not trusting in him completely.

As Pastor Henry concluded the service and invited the church to come forward and welcome the new Christians into their fellowship, Kate was struck by the idea that this wasn't over. God still had plenty of work for her to do. She began to understand that her life's work had just begun.

Chapter 13

After supper was over and the table had been cleared, Mrs. Knight took Kate and Chris into the family room for an impromptu women's Bible study, leaving Mr. Knight, Brad, and John in the living room. Mr. Knight was sitting in his chair while Brad and John sat on the couch. They were finishing off their iced tea as they watched the game. During a break, John put his glass on the coffee table and decided to ask a question that had bothered him since he had first talked to Kate.

"Mr. Knight, I have a question that I think you can help me with."

"Sure, what's up?"

"When I first met Kate, I got the impression that you knew where she was and who she was with."

"Of course, well, at least in a general sense anyway."

"Didn't it bother you that she was hanging out with a group of drunks? I mean the bunch of us aren't exactly who I would think you would want your daughter to have for friends."

"Well, it did bother me some, at first, but I trust Kate, and I believe that she has a firm grip on her faith. I had to believe that she wasn't going to do anything stupid. I did feel a whole lot better about the whole thing when she came home and started talking about how she thought she might be able to lead some of you to Christ. The more information I got from her about you, the better I felt about the whole situation."

"Honestly," Brad said, "I don't really care about the reasons. I'm just happy that things worked out the way they did."

John picked up his glass and took a drink before he continued. "I'm glad things worked out the way they did too. What I don't understand, though, is why you were at all interested in us. Nobody else ever was. It's not as though we fit anybody's description of good people."

"John, the last commandment Jesus gave his disciples before he ascended into heaven was to go into all the world and preach the good news to all creation. What that means is that we are to share our salvation with everyone. Not just the 'good people,' or the people who are like us. Jesus ate with and taught to the sinners. If we are going to be like Jesus, then we need to do the same. Also, if you think about it, if you were already Christians, then you wouldn't have been in need of salvation. You'd already have had it."

"I guess that makes sense. What about temptations, though? I mean, I'm not Jesus; it would be very hard for me to resist the temptation to do certain things."

"It will be hard for a while, but it gets easier. The key is, when you find yourself in a position like that, you need to make a conscious decision to follow Jesus' way and not the world's. Pray that he will take care of you in those situations."

"Didn't I already do that?"

"Yes, you did, but it's not something you can do once and forget about. Becoming a Christian is a decision you make once, but living as a Christian is a decision you need to make every day."

Brad sat back and rubbed his temples. "It all sounded so simple earlier. Now it's starting to sound complicated."

"It's not really all that complicated. All you need to do is to start each day with prayer, and the decision will make itself."

"How are we supposed to know," John asked, "what it is that God wants us to do?"

"That's a question that gets a lot of people in trouble. All I can tell you is to wait and learn to listen for him. He may not speak to you directly, the way I am now, but he will let you know. Whenever you think that God is speaking or leading you in a certain direction, you need to check that against what the Bible teaches. If that direction is contrary to what the Bible teaches us, then that message isn't from God."

"I'll just have to take your word for it right now," John replied, "until I can get it all figured out for myself."

"None of us will ever figure it all out until the day we meet Jesus face-to-face, maybe not even then. Until that day, though, that Bible is the best place to start."

The three ladies were sitting around a small table in the family room. Mrs. Knight had gotten out her Bible and a devotional, and the three of them were involved in a discussion about the prophets of the Old Testament. Chris, however, was focused on the present, and found it hard to concentrate on ancient history.

She couldn't believe how much better she felt than she had just a few hours ago. It seemed as though each minute that passed brought with it even more peace. Chris still had some serious questions, however, so she decided to bring them up, even though they really had very little to do with what the devotion was supposed to be about. "Mrs. Knight, I hate to change the subject, but I could really use some advice."

"I don't know how much help I will be, but I'll do what I can," Mrs. Knight said as she laid the devotional on the table.

Chris decided that the best thing to do was to get right to the point. "For years now, I've wanted to go out with John, but I was always too scared to do anything about it. Now that I am going out with him, I don't know what I'm supposed to do about it."

"Are you asking if you should sleep with him?"

"No, not really. John and I talked some about that this morning, and we both agreed that's not going to happen anytime soon. There's a lot more to it than that. The thing is, I don't really have any place to go. My mom kicked me out, and I really don't want to live in my uncle's house anyway, and there is no way that I could afford a place on my own right now. For all intents and purposes, the only home I have now is out at the farm with John. I even have my own room there. But now it just doesn't seem like the right thing to do."

"Well, you've made the right decision about sleeping with John. God wants us to wait until we're married. As far as staying in John's house, I'm not sure I know what to tell you. I sort of understand your position, but living with him, even if you do have your own room, would lead to a great deal of temptation that I don't think you're ready to face yet. You're still new to the faith, and it's not really a good idea to test it so early. Even people who have been Christians for years aren't prepared to face that sort of temptation. Are you going to go to college?"

"I really sort of doubt it. There is just no way I can afford the tuition, and my grades weren't good enough for any sort of scholarship."

Kate, who really hadn't said much since supper, put her hand on Chris's. "What about staying with April? Didn't I hear something about that?"

"I guess I could do that, but her parents don't really like me that well. I sort of doubt that would work for anyone."

"Well, I suppose you could stay here for a couple of days. I'd have to talk to Joe about it, but I don't think it would be a problem. That would give the three of us some time to figure something else out."

Chris was suddenly overwhelmed by all that had happened. There were tears in her eyes when she spoke again. "Do you really think I can do this? I don't know if I'm strong enough."

Mrs. Knight got up and went over to where Chris was sitting and wrapped her arms around her. "I know you can do this. Whenever you feel like you're being overwhelmed by life, just remember that God is there to help you through it. Kate and I will be here to help as well. Anytime you need us, just ask."

Chris wiped a tear from her eye, and hugged back. "It's been a long time since I've been comfortable talking with anyone like this. I always wished for a real family. Would it bother you any if I sort of adopted yours?"

Mrs. Knight released Chris so that she could look directly into Chris's eyes. "You already have. More than that, though, you've been adopted into the family of God."